Stand Up, Lucy

Stand Up, Lucy

By ELIZABETH HALL

Illustrated by Beth and Joe Krush

Houghton Mifflin Company Boston 1971

Also by
ELIZABETH HALL
Phoebe Snow

For my mother

I

With a clatter of hoofs and of iron wheels, the shiny red dray slid up to the curb. Will Snow tossed the reins into the street and leaped down. He ran along the walk and across the porch, two steps at a time.

"Maud, Maud," he shouted, long before he reached the house. "Maud, where are you?"

The commotion jerked Lucy away from her book and back into the world of 1904. Meg and Jo and Beth and Amy fled into the tattered copy of *Little Women* at the sight of Father running toward the house at ten o'clock on Saturday morning. Never did he come home before noon and never in her life had she seen him run. It must be something terrible.

The book slipped from her lap and landed on the floor with a bang. It lay open, the pages fluttering,

1

while she jumped up from the window seat and ran across the parlor. She reached the hall just as Mother came out of the kitchen, wiping her floury hands on her apron. Sam slid down the banister from the second floor, landing on his feet at the very moment that Father threw open the door.

"Whatever is the matter, Will?" asked Mother.

Father leaned against the door and gasped for breath. He shook his head. "I can't talk," he said. "Bring me water."

Not waiting to be told, Lucy ran to the kitchen and filled a glass. Back she went, in such a hurry that water splashed all the way across the dining room floor.

Father was sitting in the big parlor chair, Sam on one side of him and Mother on the other. He took the water, drank it in one long gulp, and handed Mother the empty glass.

She waited until he had recovered his breath. "Now," she said, "what's this all about?"

"It's," Father began, "it's . . ." He swallowed and tried again. "It's Letitia," he said. Then he stopped, reached into his pocket and pulled out a piece of yellow paper. "Here," he said, shoving it at Mother. "You read it."

Mother unfolded the square of paper and read the telegram to herself, her lips slowly forming each word. As her eyes moved down the page, her hand stole up and pressed at the base of her throat.

Lucy waited to hear what was in the telegram, but not a word passed Mother's lips. Her mouth was clamped shut and she looked from the sheet of paper to Father and back again. Father had a wild look on his face. They stared at each other.

It must be terrible. She could remember only two telegrams ever coming to the Snow house: once when Grandmother Snow died and once when Uncle Dan was in California. And, she suddenly remembered, there was one other time. The time she was sent to visit relatives, but instead had stayed on the train and gone to the great St. Louis Fair without permission. That time Aunt Amy wired Mother when she failed to get off in Clarkstown.

Mother finally parted her lips. She was about to speak. Lucy and Sam leaned forward to catch every word. Now, at last, they would hear the news.

"After all these years," said Mother, "I just don't understand."

"Don't understand what?" asked Sam. It was almost a howl.

"Who sent it?" asked Lucy. "Was it Uncle Dan?"

"I'm sorry," said Mother. She read the telegram again, aloud:

ARRIVING SUNDAY 2:45 P.M. STOP PLEASE MEET TRAIN STOP YOUR SISTER, LETITIA

"Beats me," said Father. "I haven't seen Letitia in twenty-three years. Eighteen and eighty-one it was

3

when she packed her bags and said she'd had enough of small towns." His voice softened. He shook his head. "Never even sent us a Christmas card after the first year. Like to broke Mother's heart."

And now she was coming back to Smithville. Lucy had heard many tales of Aunt Letitia's childhood. The way Father told it, his sister's whole life had been devoted to outwitting her parents and persecuting her little brother.

But all the tales stopped with Aunt Letitia's eighteenth birthday. Something scandalous must have happened after that, because when she asked Father about it, he turned red and mumbled that she wouldn't be interested. Today was the first time she had heard that Aunt Letitia lived in New York. And tomorrow her mysterious aunt would be in this very house.

She glanced at her brother. She could almost see the wheels turning inside that carrot-colored head.

"How long do you suppose she'll stay?" asked Mother.

"No way to tell," said Father. He looked uneasily from Lucy to Sam. "No way to tell," he repeated.

"Shall I put her in the front bedroom?" asked Mother.

Father looked at the floor, then up the stairs, then at Mother. "I don't think so," he said. "If she stays just a night or two, I don't mind giving up my bed." He forced his lips into a weak smile. "But we don't know

4

how long she'll be here." His voice grew firmer. "Better give her the back bedroom," he said.

He got up, put on his hard brown hat, rebuttoned his coat and walked across the parlor. At the door he stopped, came back and kissed Mother on the cheek.

"Don't worry, Maud," he said. "It'll work out." Then he was gone.

Mother stared after him. The front door closed but she did not move until the sound of horses seemed to waken her. She frowned and rubbed her forehead. A streak of flour traced the path of her fingers.

"Lucy," she said, "go upstairs and open the windows in the back bedroom."

"Can't it wait?" asked Lucy. "I have to work on my speech."

In just over a week, Smithville High School would hold class elections, and she hoped to be elected secretary of the ninth grade. On Wednesday she would have to give a campaign speech in the school auditorium before all the students.

Mother frowned. "No, it can't," she said. "There's lots to do before your Aunt Letitia comes tomorrow, and I'm going to need your help. If we expect to have any bread, I must set the dough."

"But Mother . . ." began Lucy.

"No buts," said Mother. "You've had time to read a book. You also have plenty of time to get the spare room ready for your aunt."

Lucy tried once more. "You really don't want Aunt Letitia to visit us," she said. "Why do we have to make everything so nice?"

Now Mother sounded cross. "She's your father's sister," she said. "Her room will be as nice as we can make it. I don't want to hear another excuse. Run upstairs and open those windows."

As they talked, Sam walked quietly toward the door. "Sam," called Mother. Her voice caught him before he could get away. "You can help turn that mattress."

His small shoulders sagged. Behind Mother's back Lucy stuck out her tongue at her brother. At least she would have company in her misery.

Sam followed her up the stairs. It was months since anyone had been in the spare bedroom at the end of the hall. Unless company came, it was opened only at spring-cleaning time, when brooms and mops and dustcloths and strong-smelling ammonia water chased away the ghosts of winter.

She knew there were no such things as ghosts, so the room could not be haunted. But each time she entered, she half-expected a shadowy figure to jump out of the carved wardrobe where Mother stored unused clothing. It was almost eight feet tall with heavy wood doors and looked very much like the wardrobes she read about in ghost stories. Three men could easily stand side-by-side in it, so there was surely room for a single spectral tenant.

6

When she turned the knob, the door swung open with a creak. Inside it was cold and dark and musty. There had been no heat in the room since the summer sun gave way to the frosts of autumn.

Lucy groped her way to the window, keeping as far away from the wardrobe as she could. Sam waited in the lighted hall. She raised the shades and objects in the room lost their air of mystery in the morning sun. When she threw open the glass, she shivered at the icy air that rushed in.

"It's safe to come in now," she said over her shoulder.

Sam stepped inside. "I was just keeping out of your way," he said.

He picked up one side of the mattress and pulled while Lucy pushed from the other side. They tugged and shoved at the lumpy pad. Once they had it on end, Sam paused in his struggles.

"What do you think she looks like?" he asked.

"How should I know," said Lucy. "I've never seen a picture of her. Like Father, I guess."

She thought for a moment. "There are some ancient pictures in this room," she said. "When we were cleaning last spring, Mother put them in the bureau drawer."

"Let's get this old thing turned so we can look at them," said Sam. His voice became hushed. "Do you suppose she's a scarlet woman?" he asked.

She blinked. "Sam Snow," she said, "do you even know what a scarlet woman is?" This was too much.

Her brother was only ten, and when she was his age she certainly had never heard of such creatures.

He gave the mattress a push with his shoulder and it flopped over. "Aw, they're something terrible, I guess," he said. "Jerry Martin said scarlet women were wicked. And Walter Smith said that New York was full of them."

"Don't worry about things that are beyond you," said Lucy.

Sam pulled out the top drawer and began to rummage around, scattering old photographs over the bureau.

She watched him for a while, then said impatiently, "You'll never find it that way. Let me help."

Lucy picked up a stack of pictures. Each was framed behind glass. Some were square, some were long and one was oval. She looked at the oval first. Father and Mother on their wedding day. Father sat very stiff in a straight chair and Mother stood beside him, her hand on his shoulder. Neither of them smiled. They looked very young.

Sam went through the other pictures. There was one of Lucy as a baby in a long, white dress that covered her feet, and an old one of Sam, his hair in spiral ringlets.

Sam tried to slip it under the rest of the stack.

"Look at the little girl in the pretty sailor suit," she said. "Isn't she cute!"

8

"Aw, I was only two years old then," Sam said.

Lucy examined the next picture. It was stained and faded and dog-eared, but there was no mistake. Below the image was written, in pale brown ink, "Letitia Snow, age 16." A beautiful young girl smiled out at her, yards of gauzy material about her shoulders and a single strand of pearls around her neck.

"Here it is!" said Lucy.

Sam dropped the other pictures into the drawer and peered over Lucy's shoulder. He whistled. "Aunt Letitia's a looker!" he said. "She could even be a stage actress."

"She's as pretty as the girls in the advertisements," said Lucy. "Now we'll recognize her at the train tomorrow." She put the pictures away and shut the bureau drawer. The prospect of meeting her aunt suddenly seemed attractive.

She opened the door of the walnut commode and took out the china washbowl and pitcher. Once more she admired the yellow and pink rosebuds that twined across the surface. She had chosen them herself from the Sears, Roebuck catalog. She held them out to Sam.

"Here," she said, "take these downstairs so that Mother can wash them."

As he took them, the pitcher rattled against the bowl and Lucy gave him a sharp glance.

"Don't break them," she said.

"You're just great at ordering people around," he said.

9

"If you're elected class secretary, I pity the poor students."

Out the door he ran before Lucy could think of a suitable retort. She sighed and leaned her cheek against the cold brass bedpost. Brothers were terrible nuisances. Before long she had forgotten him and forgotten Aunt Letitia. She imagined herself writing neat letters in black ink with her best penmanship and signing them Lucy Snow, Class Secretary.

In only a week, in nine days, Smithville High School would hold its elections.

II

Father snapped shut the case of his railroad watch. "She's six minutes and twenty-seven seconds late," he announced. "But they can make up that time before they reach Clarkstown."

The Calumet Special stood at the Smithville station. It sighed like a great animal and jets of steam hissed from the black engine. Drops of water fell onto the earth beside the shining rails.

Lucy looked down the length of the train, eager for her first glimpse of beautiful Aunt Letitia. Would her hair be a flaming red like Father's or the orange of ripe carrots like Sam's or would it be a rich auburn like Lucy's own thick braids? Her eyes swept past the lone woman with gray hair who climbed down from the

11

second car. Perhaps Aunt Letitia had missed her train in New York.

Then Father brushed by her and strode across the platform. "Letitia!" he called.

Lucy could scarcely believe her eyes. The gray-haired woman broke into a smile.

"Will!" she exclaimed.

"Gee whillikers!" said Sam as he watched Father sweep the woman into his arms. "Is that Aunt Letitia?"

No one answered. They all watched as Aunt Letitia put up a hand to keep her hat from falling to the ground. She stepped back and peered at Father through gold-rimmed spectacles.

"I'd know you anywhere, Will," she said. "But twenty-three years ago you didn't have that mustache."

Father took his sister's arm and brought her over to the platform. As they neared, Mother smoothed her skirt, touched her hair and put on her best company smile. All through the introductions, Lucy watched her aunt closely. Aunt Letitia's face looked as if it had been chiseled out of strong granite. A black plush cape embroidered with braid and jet beads covered the top of her rusty black dress. A spray of bedraggled feathers stuck out of the ugly black hat that rode squarely on her head. A small black leather bag hung by a gilt chain from her belt. In her hand she carried a black umbrella with a curved silver handle, which was shaped like a parrot's head.

Aunt Letitia kissed Mother politely on the cheek and shook Sam's hand, but when she was introduced to Lucy, the granite cheeks softened in a warm smile.

She clasped both of Lucy's hands and said, "You've produced a real woman, Will. She reminds me of myself at sixteen or seventeen or eighteen."

Lucy smiled back with delight, but Mother's eyes widened and she looked at Father. He ran his finger along the inside of his stiff collar.

"She's only fourteen, Letitia," he said. "Only fourteen."

"But as tall as Maud," said Aunt Letitia.

With visible discomfort Father glanced around the station. "You must have a bag," he said. "I'll send Sam over to fetch it."

"That won't do, Will," said Aunt Letitia. "It'll take more than Sam to get my things."

She pointed toward the baggage car, where two men struggled with an enormous trunk bound with steel bands. Another trunk, every bit as large, sat on the ground beside the train.

"That's all yours?" asked Father. His voice rose sharply with each word.

"Part of it," she said.

The second trunk settled beside the first and the corner of a third appeared in the door of the baggage car. Mother's hand flew up to cover her mouth and Father began to chew on his mustache.

"I'll move the dray over," he said. He almost ran toward the shiny red wagon with black wheels.

Father drove the town dray and delivered all the goods that came into Smithville by rail. Every spool of thread, every shoe, every cup and plate sold at Harrison's Mercantile first rode from the station to the store on the back of Father's dray. Every bottle of castor oil, every bar of soap and every jar of hair restorer sold at the drugstore had been carried by Father. Not a can of food or bag of coffee left the grocery that had not first been handled by Father. His dray and the fine pair of horses that pulled it were his pride and he often said that his job was as important to the town as Banker Smith's.

He coaxed Saint and Sinner, the two big horses, into position beside the baggage car and climbed down from his narrow seat. He bent to lift the first trunk and straightened, leaving the luggage on the ground. There was a puzzled expression on his face.

"This thing must be loaded with rocks," he said.

The stationmaster came over and together they managed to hoist the large trunk into the dray. Twice more they strained and panted until the other two trunks had joined the first. The stationmaster walked slowly back toward his office, one hand clasped over the small of his back. Though it was a cold October day, beads of sweat stood out on Father's forehead. He mopped his brow with a large handkerchief and bravely waved to the family.

Sam and Lucy scrambled into the back of the dray. Even loaded with three large trunks, there was still plenty of room for them to sit comfortably with their legs stretched out.

Father helped Mother up into the seat, then he gave a hand to Aunt Letitia. As she climbed into the wagon, her skirt caught on the big front wheel. Before she could unhook it, Sam nudged Lucy and pointed. Above the slim ankle was the flounce of a red ruffled petticoat.

"So that's what they mean by a scarlet woman," said Sam. "Wait till I tell Jerry."

"You'll do nothing of the kind," said Lucy in a sharp whisper, her eyes caught by the red taffeta ruffle.

It was the first red petticoat she had ever seen. Once she had found a red petticoat advertised in the big Sears catalog, but Mother had been shocked when she suggested that they add it to their order.

Perhaps Aunt Letitia was not as grim as she appeared.

Father walked around the wagon and climbed up on the driver's side. The seat was so crowded that he had to dangle his leg over the edge. He shook the reins and called out. Saint started obediently, but Sinner jerked his black head and whinnied. Father spoke sharply and the horses pulled together and the dray rolled away from the station.

Sam crawled over to where Lucy sat, her back against one of the black enameled trunks.

"How old do you figure she is?" he whispered into her ear.

Lucy thought for a moment. "Aunt Letitia is five years older than Father," she said slowly, "so that makes her forty-three."

"She looks more like sixty," he said. "Her hair is all gray and that old dress and hat make her look like a grandma."

Lucy thought of the red ruffled petticoat and smiled. "She's not as old as you think," she said.

"I hope not," said Sam. "With all those trunks she brought, she might stay forever." He scowled and crawled back to his side of the dray.

Lucy watched the station recede in the distance and thought about her aunt. She was willing to bet that things were going to be different around the Snow household.

III

THE CLOCK at the front of the schoolroom softly chimed the quarter hour. Lucy looked up from her algebra book. Only five minutes since she had cast her last imploring look at the black and white face. Fifteen minutes before the hands would rescue her from another weary battle with x and y.

She looked at Mr. Chester who sat behind his desk and pursed his narrow lips as he turned the pages of a book. His high-domed forehead rose above his round spectacles, and his forelocks were carefully combed over his bald head. Lucy wondered how he looked when he first woke up in the morning, with that hair hanging down over his ears and his skull gleaming in the sunlight.

She chewed her pencil and once again stared at the problem. But the age of John, who was twice as old as his brother and one-third as old as his mother, remained a mysterious x. Her head was full of next week's election.

Only eight days ago Tom Bryan had come to her with the idea. He was a candidate for class treasurer and he said it would be fun for them to hold office together.

Tom lived just a block from Lucy and sometimes they walked to school together. On Sunday afternoons, he often came home from church with the Snows and spent the afternoon playing Parcheesi or checkers with Sam and Lucy.

Now it was hard to think of anything except the election. But instead of spending her time on ideas for posters and speeches and ways to convince people she would be the best secretary in Smithville High, she found herself dreaming about the job.

Sometimes she saw herself as a typewriter, one of those ladies who sat in an office all day and wrote letters by punching keys. At other times she imagined herself being excused from algebra to meet important visitors. This time she saw herself conducting an emergency meeting of the ninth grade, when both the class president and vice president were ill with grippe. As she raised the gavel to call the meeting to order, someone spoke.

18

"Having trouble, Miss Snow? Perhaps you see the answers to algebra problems dancing on the lawn amid the autumn leaves?"

The voice of Mr. Chester banished the upturned faces that waited for the rap of Lucy's gavel. She turned flaming cheeks to her algebra and pretended not to hear the laughter of the class. Gradually the aimless figures began to march in neat rows across the paper. By the time the school bell clanged, she had discovered that John was ten, just the age of her own brother.

Lucy gathered her books and put on her sweater without once glancing at the front of the room where Mr. Chester sat quietly at his desk, waiting for the class to return to order. At last he gave the word and around her rose the clatter of the school day's close — the shuffling feet, the dropped books and the chatter of her classmates.

Tom stopped beside her desk. "Old Chester is in a bad mood today," he said.

She smiled at him. "He certainly got after me," she said. Tom's words soothed her injured pride.

As they walked down the steps, he turned to her. "Have you finished your speech?" he asked. "The assembly is tomorrow."

Lucy shook her head. "No," she said. "My Aunt Letitia arrived on Sunday, and we spent the weekend getting ready for her. I've made a few notes, but I haven't written them out."

Gold and brown leaves tumbled before a sudden gust of wind. As it bit into her back, she huddled inside her sweater and wished that she had worn her heavy coat.

"You'll do all right," said Tom. "I've never known you to be at a loss for words." He took her books and carried them easily in the crook of his arm. "Now put your hands in your pockets before they freeze," he said.

Lucy obediently tucked her fingers into her pockets but took them out again to nudge Tom.

"Look at that!" she said.

Pasted to the fence at the corner was a big white poster proclaiming in black letters:

A SISTER WILL SPEAK FOR WOMEN
SMITHVILLE CITY PARK
THURSDAY, OCTOBER 20, 1904
7:30 P.M.
STAND UP FOR WOMEN'S RIGHTS!!!

From one corner of the placard smiled a fashionable lady, a dimple in the corner of her pretty mouth and a string of pearls around her slim neck.

"Just think," she said, "a suffragist right here in Smithville."

Lucy had never seen a suffragist, one of those females who traveled around the country, urging that women be given the vote. But she had heard talk about such apostles of equal rights. Father called them unnatural and the Devil's own helpers, out to upset the balance of nature. Now one of these strange creatures was coming to Smithville!

Tom looked puzzled. "What in the world is a suffragist?" he asked.

Lucy remembered what Father had said when she asked him the same question after he had delivered a lengthy lecture on the evils of woman suffrage. "Suffrage is the right to vote in political matters," she repeated, "and a suffragist is a woman who tries to persuade men to let all women have that right."

"Oh, yes," said Tom, "those crazy women who run around and chain themselves to ballot boxes. I've heard of them, all right."

For several minutes they stood without talking while Tom studied the poster.

"Do you suppose anybody will go?" he asked.

"Of course they'll go," said Lucy. "I'm going." She nodded her red head. "I wouldn't miss it for the world."

"I'd like to be there when you tell your Father," said Tom. "He'll explode like a skyrocket."

"I'll be there," she said. "Just wait."

Despite her brave words, Lucy had no idea how she would get to the park. Father would never listen to a suffragist for five seconds, let alone make a trip across town to hear one. Will Snow was a man of decided opinions, none of them kept to himself, and he consigned suffragists to the pit, along with Democrats.

Lucy ran the last block from Tom's house, hurried

up the steps and banged open the front door. Dropping her books on the hall table beside Sam's fat red arithmetic book and *Blue-Backed Speller,* she went into the kitchen.

The large room was warm; lard heated in a black iron skillet on top of the big woodburning stove. She glanced at the woodbox beside the stove, then relaxed. Sam had filled the box before he went out to play. Sometimes he slipped away and left it empty, and then she had to bring in an armload of wood herself.

"Where's Aunt Letitia?" she asked.

Mother looked up from the chicken she was coating with flour. "Aunt Letitia went out at two o'clock," she answered. "Said she would be back in time for supper." She turned the chicken leg. "Did you have a good day at school?" she said.

"It was all right," said Lucy. She wanted to forget Mr. Chester's sarcasm. She washed her hands at the sink and tied a checkered apron around her waist. "What can I do to help?" she asked.

"You can peel those potatoes," said Mother, "and cut them into pieces so they'll cook quickly." She smiled and went back to flouring chicken. Whenever Lucy offered to help, there was sure to be a plan afoot. And her imagination sometimes ran wild.

For some time they worked in silence, then Lucy stopped gouging the eyes from a large potato. "Mother," she said and fell silent. She carefully cut out another eye and began again. This time the words tumbled out so fast they all ran together. "There's a suffragist speaking in the park on Thursday evening. Will you take me?"

"You know how your Father feels about suffragists," said Mother. "He'd never let you go."

Lucy picked up another potato. Her knife pared away a thick strip of skin as she said, "Do we have to tell Father we're going?"

"You're peeling that potato away, Lucy," said Mother. She dropped a chicken wing into the flour and turned it, then picked up another.

"Thursday night is choir night," said Lucy. "If we don't say anything about the meeting in the park, he won't tell us we *can't* go."

Mother dropped the first pieces of chicken into the bubbling lard. Looking intently at the frying pan, she said, "If Father asks us where we are going, we must tell him the truth."

"Of course! Oh, thank you, Mother," said Lucy. She threw her arms around Mother and squeezed hard. Mother never disobeyed Father, but she occasionally forgot to tell him about something she knew he would forbid. It saved many arguments.

IV

Father folded his *New York Times* and laid it on the side table. Although it was three days old and he had read the news once before in the *Smithville Courier*, he never felt well informed until he had digested the *Times'* version of a story.

"Those brazen suffragettes are invading Smithville," he said. "Some city dude plastered posters all over town. When he tried to put one up at the railroad station, I told him a thing or two.

"Yes," Father continued, "he decided that he didn't really need a poster at the station. Just shriveled up and slunk away when I told him how the cow ate the cabbage." Father stroked his red mustache.

Sam paid no attention. Curled up in a big chair, his

rusty head bent over a copy of *The Jungle Book*, he ran beside Mowgli and Bagheera in the jungles of India. But Lucy raised her eyes and silently pleaded with Mother.

Aunt Letitia looked up from her knitting. Her eyes on Father, she looped the dark blue yarn around the needles without missing a stitch.

"Told him you owned the railroad, did you?" she asked.

The only sound was the click, click of her needles. Mother put her hand to her lips. Father opened his mouth and closed it again. He shifted uneasily in his chair.

"I told him how the good people of this town felt about suffragettes," he said. His voice grew stronger. "He needn't think anyone in Smithville would go listen to one of those shameless females."

The needles clicked even faster.

"I'm sure you convinced him, dear," said Mother. She placed her basket of darning on the sofa and stood up. "Would anyone care for a piece of warm apple pie? Lucy, you come help me."

Lucy closed her book and followed Mother into the kitchen. It had been a narrow escape. Father's next words might well forbid her to go hear the speech. As she entered the kitchen, she heard Father say, over the sound of the needles, "That woman will get up on her soapbox and there won't be a soul come to hear her."

While the pie warmed in the oven, Mother cut thick

slices of crumbly, golden cheese. Lucy put five plates on the counter, then turned, the forks held tightly in her hand.

"What if the preacher asks us on Sunday why we weren't at choir practice?" she said.

"We'll tell him we went to hear the suffragist," said Mother in a firm but quiet voice.

"But what if Father is standing next to us when Mr. Hinckley asks?" Lucy's voice trembled.

"That's a chance you just have to take, Lucy." Mother slid the pie from the oven and topped each fat, juicy wedge with a slice of cheese. "Now give this pie to your father and to Sam," she said. "I can handle three."

Father smiled broadly when Lucy handed him his plate. "I like any kind of pie," he said with a chuckle, "as long as it's apple."

Sam put his book aside and grabbed his plate from Lucy. But he waited until Mother brought Lucy's plate before he began to eat — not out of courtesy or kindness, but because he wanted to be certain his piece was at least as large as his sister's.

Aunt Letitia put down her knitting and cut into her pie. "Lucy," she said, "what's this I hear about you running for class secretary?"

Lucy leaned back in her chair. Her aunt had steered the conversation into calmer waters. "The election is next Monday," she answered. "Tomorrow is the big assembly and I have to make a speech."

"A good campaign speech is very important," said Father seriously. "I hope yours is all ready."

"I've made notes," said Lucy, "and I know what I want to say."

"The best speeches are made that way," said Aunt Letitia. "If you have to read your speech, you lose your audience."

"Lucy's running against that stuck-up Mabel Smith," said Sam. "She thinks she's so smart because her father owns the bank. Maybe she'll try to win by giving away free samples." His voice changed to a squeaky falsetto. "Please accept this little greenback as a token of my appreciation and don't forget to vote for me on Monday."

"That's not nice," said Mother. But there was a twinkle in her eye.

"According to the *Courier*," said Father, "there'll be some real excitement in Smithville next week. The Republicans are going to stage a torchlight parade for Teddy Roosevelt and Senator Throckmorton will speak."

"Can we go? Can we go?" asked Sam, his mouth full of pie. "Can we?"

"Don't talk with your mouth stuffed," said Father. "Indeed we'll go. A presidential election is an important thing. You'll be voting yourself one day and you should learn how politics works."

"Guess Mother and Lucy and Aunt Letitia won't have to go," said Sam, as he scraped the last bit of pie from his plate. "They'll never get to vote." He grinned triumphantly at Lucy.

She choked on her pie.

"Women may not vote," said Father, "but that's no reason to deprive them of the privilege of seeing a United States Senator. Of course the ladies will go."

"Girls are just too dumb to vote," said Sam, unable to resist another thrust at his sister.

Lucy could not restrain herself. "You should talk," she said, shaking her finger at Sam. "We all know who has to have help on his long division every night."

"We'll have no more of that," said Father. "There's really a very practical reason why women should not vote. They would always vote just as their husbands told them. So the only effect of woman suffrage would be to double the cost of holding an election. And that would mean higher taxes."

Across the room the knitting needles clicked, clicked like a train making up time.

Father put his empty plate on the table. "My, but that was fine pie," he said. "There's nobody bakes pie like your mother."

"I know how we could reduce taxes," said Aunt Letitia.

"How's that?" asked Father, sighing with satisfaction.

"Simple," she said. "Let the heads of the parties do all the voting. The Republicans and the Democrats always vote just as their leaders tell them — like silly sheep. Look at all the money we'd save."

"Don't be ridiculous, Letitia," said Father. "This is a democracy. Every man must have his say in government."

Aunt Letitia looked at Father through her gold-rimmed spectacles. "You seem to think saving money is a good reason to keep the vote from women," she said. "I thought I'd help you save a little more."

Father chewed on his mustache and looked from one member of the family to another. Aunt Letitia smiled slyly and began counting stitches. Mother's darning suddenly required all her attention. Lucy found a hangnail and picked at it with intense concentration. Only Sam did not notice the sparks that flew between Father and Aunt Letitia.

"Suppose there's any more pie in the kitchen?" he asked.

Mother spoke up quickly. "Not at this hour, young man. I don't intend to be up with you half the night."

"And speaking of long division," said Father, "have you finished your homework, Sam?"

"Aw, I was going to do it in the morning," said Sam. Slowly he got up and just as slowly came back with his school books. He sat down at the table and stared at the open arithmetic book and the sheet of blank paper.

Lucy gathered up the soiled plates and forks. As she went to the kitchen, she looked back over her shoulder at Sam. The crisis was over and her secret was safe. And Sam was miserable. It served him right.

V

Lᴜᴄʏ ᴡᴀʟᴋᴇᴅ into the school auditorium and took a deep breath. The familiar odor of dust and tennis shoes excited her. She remembered the plays, the puppet shows and the magicians she had seen. And the lectures and speeches and the music she had heard. Each time she came here, she felt that something special was about to happen.

All the candidates for class offices sat together in the first two rows. Lucy sat down in the only empty seat and looked up at the yellow ringlets of Mabel Smith.

"Hello, Mabel," said Lucy. Her smile felt stiff, as if it had been pasted on her face.

"Oh, it's you. Hello," said Mabel. There was no smile on Mabel's lips and her voice was sharp and cold. She looked away and stared at the empty stage, her nose faintly wrinkled as if she smelled a crock of souring cream.

The smile disappeared from Lucy's face. Just because her father was the banker was no reason for Mabel to be so stuck-up. They had never been friends, but there was no reason to be rude. In the midst of the laughter and whispering, a circle of silence surrounded the girls.

The room grew quiet as Mr. Amberson walked briskly onto the stage. He cleared his throat and began to discuss the class elections.

Lucy heard hardly a word. Each time she saw Mr. Amberson she could only stare with fascination at his incredible eyebrows. The school principal was a kind man, with twinkling dark eyes, a bald, shiny head and a round nose like Santa Claus. But the shelf of his bushy eyebrows projected at least an inch into space.

Mr. Amberson ended his description of the "fine boys and girls who wish to represent their fellow students" and called Joe McBroom to the stage. Joe stood up, dropped his speech and scrambled on the floor for the scattered pages. As he went up the steps, he tripped and almost fell. At last, red-faced, he stepped to the front of the stage and waited for the laughter to stop. Then he stuttered his way through a speech extolling his virtues as the next treasurer of the ninth grade.

Joe finished, mopped his brow and left the stage. Tom was the other candidate for treasurer, and Mr. Amberson called out his name. Tom's speech was full of schemes to make money for the ninth grade class. Though he tripped over his tongue once or twice, his voice was steady and he never appeared to be frightened.

While Tom gave his speech, Lucy's eyes wandered to Mabel, whose yellow curls were dangling over something she held in her lap. She craned her neck to see what caught Mabel's attention and discovered, to her dismay, that Mabel's speech was a professional-looking typed document.

Then Mabel's name was called. She walked in front of the seats. A long pair of legs stretched across her path. She scowled and jerked her hand crossly at the boy who owned the offending legs. Then she seemed to change her mind. A syrupy smile spread over her face and she whispered a few words. The legs pulled back and Lucy could hear her "Thank you."

Mabel walked gracefully to the stairs, her head high, and mounted to the stage. When the room was silent again, she began to read from the pages in her hand. "Classmates of Smithville High, I come before you to ask your support in my campaign for ninth grade secretary. My decision to run for this office was based on long and careful consideration."

She delivered her speech without a single mistake. It was plain that she had practiced it many times before. That made Lucy uneasy, for she had done no more than scrawl a few notes on slips of paper. It was even plainer that Mabel's father had written the speech and that his secretary had typed it carefully. That made Lucy angry. And the longer she listened to the haughty voice reading the perfectly phrased and typed sentences, the angrier she became.

With a final, flowery phrase Mabel ended her speech. She smiled sweetly at the audience and then at Mr. Amberson and walked off the stage amid loud applause from the packed auditorium.

The principal was so impressed that he forgot that he was supposed to be impartial. "That was a very fine speech, young lady," he said. "You obviously took your assignment seriously and spent a good many hours on it." Then he looked at the paper in his hand and loudly called Lucy's name.

Lucy stood up and walked toward the stairs.

The space between the stage and the first row of seats was just wide enough for the two girls to pass shoulder to shoulder. They met in the center of the passageway. Lucy stepped to the right at the same moment as Mabel, then both girls stepped to the left. For several seconds they continued this dance, moving from one side to the other accompanied by steadily increased laughter from the audience. Then Lucy somehow slipped by and hurried up the steps.

As she waited for the laughter to die down, Lucy looked out over the audience. There was Tom winking at her from the first row. And the girl who sat across from her in algebra waved confidently.

At last the room was quiet. She thrust her hand into her dress pocket for her notes. Slowly she drew out her clenched fist and looked at it in wonder. Her pocket was empty. Uneasily she reached into her sweater. Nothing there except a handkerchief. The other pocket yielded only a lint-covered hoarhound drop.

By now a restless shuffling of feet had spread through the room. In desperation, Lucy once again tried her dress. She remembered putting those notes in her pocket. They had to be there. Suddenly, an image appeared as clearly as if it had been thrown onto a screen by a magic lantern. She saw herself standing before a mirror that very morning, shaking her head and changing her dress. All her notes were at home, in the pocket of the blue dress that hung in her closet.

A rustle of whispers began as Lucy stared at the crowd in panic. She could think of nothing to say. She opened her mouth but nothing came out. She thought a moment and tried again, but it was no use. She was so angry at Mabel and her ghostwritten speech that she could think of nothing to say. At last she gasped, "Please vote for me for ninth grade secretary. I think I would do a good job."

She hurried off the stage to mingled applause and laughter. Whistles came from the back of the room.

"You tell 'em, Lucy," shouted a deep voice.

The noise followed her all the way down the steps and across the room. Not until Mr. Amberson strode out onto the stage and raised his arms for silence did the hoots and snickers die down.

Once more in her hard, wooden seat, Lucy squirmed. Though the speeches went on for another forty minutes, she might have been at home. Her cheeks burned and tears of embarrassment filled her eyes. For all practical purposes, the election for class secretary was over. There was no doubt that she had lost. And it was all her own fault.

VI

As she walked slowly out of the auditorium Lucy felt a hand on her arm. She turned to find Tom, who had stopped to wait for her.

"It was just awful," she said, blinking back the tears.

They stood in front of the door. A stream of students poured out of the school and flowed around them. Tom pulled her aside.

"It's not as bad as all that," he said. His brown eyes were kind. "At least you didn't run on forever. Lucy Snow, girl orator, shortest speeches east of the Mississippi."

Lucy couldn't smile. "Mabel sounded like Teddy Roosevelt," she said. "She had them eating out of her hand. I might as well give up now." Suddenly she remembered that Tom had given his own speech. "But you were wonderful," she said.

"It did go pretty well, but I practiced a lot," said Tom. "My father said if he heard me say 'Fellow Students' one more time he was going to walk out of the house and stay away until after the election."

"I should have practiced," said Lucy, "but I didn't even write a speech. And then I left my notes at home." She began to walk slowly away from the auditorium. "I just elected Mabel secretary."

Tom grasped her arm and forced her to stop. "Don't put on so," he said. "The election isn't over. Mabel hasn't won yet."

"Let's stop talking about it," said Lucy. "We don't want to be the last ones on the school grounds." She straightened her shoulders and marched off, determined not to think about her speech or about Mabel.

They walked down the street, kicking at the red and gold and brown leaves that littered the sidewalk. Each time Lucy saw a particularly large leaf she stepped squarely on its center, making it crackle.

When they reached the corner Tom broke the silence. He pointed to the poster at the corner of the fence. "Still going to hear your wild woman?" he asked.

"Of course I am," said Lucy. "I wouldn't miss it for anything."

Tom looked down at her. "Lucy Snow," he said,

"your father would never let you go hear a suffragist. How are you going to get out of the house?"

"Promise not to tell," said Lucy. "Not Father, not anybody. Especially not Sam."

Without waiting for his reply, she hurried on. "Well," she said, "every Thursday night Mother and I go to choir practice. And the suffragist speaks this Thursday night. We'll just leave at the usual time. Father will think we're going to church."

Tom leaned against the fence and thought for a moment. "But what if your father finds out?"

Lucy sighed impatiently, even though this was the same question she had asked Mother. "That's a chance I just have to take, Tom," she said.

"And if Sam finds out what you're planning . . ."

"He might tell," she broke in. "And even if he didn't tell, he'd make my life miserable, hinting and pretending and teasing."

"What about your aunt?" he asked.

"She's hardly ever home. She jams that old hat on her head, grabs her umbrella and flies out the door. Almost every afternoon and evening. And she never says where she's going. You should hear Father rave about women on the street alone after dark."

"Your mother is really going along?"

"Of course she is," said Lucy. "My mother thinks it's a crime that women can't vote." Mother had never once

39

hinted that she was a suffragist at heart, but it sounded impressive. And besides, Mother was going to take her to the park on Thursday.

At the sound of running feet, the conspirators drew apart. Around the corner of the fence hurtled a small body.

Tom grabbed the projectile's collar and found himself looking at Sam. He let go and stepped back. "Where do you think you're going in such a hurry?" he asked.

Sam gasped for a few seconds, then took a deep breath. "I been looking for Lucy," he said. "I have to show her something."

"I'm right here, pest," said Lucy. "Show me whatever you have to show."

"I'm only trying to do you a favor," said Sam. "If you don't want to see what I have, you don't have to look." He started to walk away, scuffing at the leaves on the walk.

Lucy called after him. "I'm sorry, Sam," she said. "You're not really a pest."

Sam put his hand in his pocket and pulled out a small white card that he thrust at Lucy. "I told you that Mabel Smith would be giving away free samples," he said.

Lucy turned the card around. She felt as if Sam had butted her in the stomach. In one corner of the small oblong was glued a shiny copper penny. Beside it, neatly lettered in black India ink, was a rhyme:

Bright as a penny,
Shiny as a dime,
Elect Mabel secretary,
She'll do fine.

Lucy swallowed hard once, then again. "Look at this," she said, as she held the card out for Tom to read.

Tom whistled. "Am I glad she's not running for treasurer," he said.

"Now she's buying votes," said Sam. "What are you going to do?"

"I guess we're lucky her father didn't give her dimes to paste on the cards," said Lucy. "Thanks, Sam. But where did you get this?" Her voice was almost cheerful.

"Walter Smith gave it to me. Mabel's going to pass them out at school tomorrow. Walter knew I'd show it to you. He hoped you'd get mad."

Lucy thought hard. Suddenly she smiled. "Tom, would you like to come over after supper and pull some taffy? Doesn't a taffy pull sound like fun?"

Two pairs of wide eyes stared at Lucy in amazement. It hardly seemed like the time to make candy.

VII

THE PAN OF MOLASSES, vinegar, butter and sugar bubbled on top of the stove. Prodded by his sister, Sam opened the door and tossed another stick of wood on the fire. Lucy dried the last supper dish and put it on the cupboard shelf. She hung the towel on a rack at the end of the sink and took a dish of butter from the icebox.

A sharp knock sent Sam to the kitchen door. There stood Tom, still wearing the puzzled look that had crossed his face at Lucy's invitation. His questions began the second he crossed the threshold.

"Will you please tell me why you decided to pull taffy this evening?" he asked.

"If you butter this for me," said Lucy, "I'll show you." She set a large platter on the kitchen table, then went into the dining room.

Tom shook his head as he washed his hands at the kitchen sink. He dipped his fingers into the mound of yellow butter. "What's your crazy sister up to now?" he asked.

"Wait and see," said Sam. He stood on his toes and took a long sniff of the boiling syrup. "I can hardly wait," he said, licking his lips. "For once in her life Lucy has a good idea. Wait till old Mabel sees this."

Lucy came back into the kitchen with a smile and a light step. She held a small card before Tom's face. "Look at this," she said, "then tell me what you think of Mabel's pennies."

Tom read the words printed on the card and shook his head once again, this time in admiration. "Lucy, you've stolen her thunder. How did you ever think of it?"

On the corner of the card was pasted a gumdrop. Boldly printed in the center of the card was a verse:

> Want a secretary
> Sweet as candy?
> Vote for Lucy,
> She'll be dandy.

"I'd like to shake your hand," said Tom. He thrust his buttery fingers at Lucy.

She skipped away from him and said, "Won't Mabel be furious when we pass out these cards with pieces of taffy fastened to them?"

"I'd just as soon have candy as a penny — any day," said Tom.

"If you two would quit playing," said Sam from his post by the stove, "I think this taffy's about ready to pull."

Lucy dashed to the sink and ran fresh, cold water into a cup. She picked up a large spoon, dipped it into the boiling candy and let a few drops of the hot syrup fall into the water. The small brown marbles sank quickly to the bottom of the cup.

She stuck her fingers in and felt them. "It's ready," she said. "This pot is heavy. Tom, would you pour the candy?"

Tom wiped his hands and took the potholder from Lucy. He lifted the pan from the stove and carried the steaming candy to the kitchen table. He tipped it carefully and a sheet of boiling syrup oozed over the edge, melting the thick coat of butter as it moved across the surface of the platter.

From the cupboard Lucy took a small bottle of peppermint oil and shook it gently above the steaming slab. Several drops fell onto the brown mass. "There!" she said. "It'll soon be cool enough to pull."

Sam snatched up the butter dish. He smeared his hands and thrust them close to his sister's face, opening and closing his fingers before her eyes.

"Stop!" shrieked Lucy, backing up against the sink.

"Settle down, Sam," said Tom, "or I'll rub your face

in the butter." He picked up the dish and Sam quickly subsided.

Lucy buttered her fingers and tested the slab of taffy. "I think it's ready."

Tom and Lucy pulled a handful of candy between them and folded it back on itself. Gradually it stiffened and changed color. With each pull it grew a shade lighter than before. Finally it became a glittering crystal ribbon.

Tom handed it to Lucy. "Now it's up to you," he said.

She molded the candy into a ball and pulled one corner out into a narrow rope that snaked across the board spread with powdered sugar. Using buttered shears, she snipped the rope into small pieces, until a satiny mound stood before them.

Sam could resist no longer. His hand darted out and snatched a glistening piece.

"Boy, is this good," he said, his words sticking together.

"Better than a penny, better than a dime, I'll take Lucy's candy any old time," said Tom. He took two of the biggest pieces.

While Lucy washed the dishes, the boys sat at the table and stuck the taffy onto the campaign cards, using egg white as glue. From time to time she left the sink to inspect their work and to make sure they didn't eat more than they fixed onto the cards.

When the task was finished, Lucy put what was left of the taffy into a cut-glass bowl, and the three made a procession into the parlor. Tom led the way, the candy held high like an offering. Lucy came next, her campaign cards piled on a silver dish that usually came out of the cupboard only at Thanksgiving to hold celery and olives. Sam brought up the rear, a pot lid in each hand. He banged the lids together at regular intervals, keeping time with a chant of "Left, right, left, right."

Father looked over the top of his newspaper. "What's all the racket?" he asked. "A man can't read his paper in peace and quiet."

Tom bowed low. "A present from the next secretary of the ninth grade," he said and held out the bowl with a flourish.

"Peppermint taffy!" said Mother. "It turned out beautifully. Smooth and cooked just long enough."

Aunt Letitia put down her knitting and inspected the cards. She took off her glasses and nodded her head as she wiped each lens. "You'll win in a walk, Lucy," she said.

"Please take one," said Lucy. She held the silver dish out to Father.

He picked up a card and looked at it. A smile spread over his face. He rubbed his nose and stroked his mustache to hide his pleasure. "Looks as if we have a politician in the family, Maud," he said. He glanced up at Lucy. "Too bad you're not a boy. I'd run you for the State Assembly."

Lucy stared at Father. She had never really thought about this before. Because she had been born a girl she could never vote; she could never run for office. But John Brooks, who sat quietly in the corner of the schoolroom and still couldn't read or multiply eight times seven after nine years of trying, would someday help choose the President — could even be President himself if enough people voted for him. And just because he was a boy. It was unfair.

VIII

Long before the bell rang, Lucy took up her post at the top of the stairs, just outside the schoolhouse door. Her campaign cards filled the cigar box she had decorated with colored paper. The morning was sunny but cold, and she was glad she had worn a warm sweater.

The early students began to arrive. As each ninth grader mounted the steps, Lucy held out the box and said, "Vote for Lucy Snow."

Joe McBroom blundered up the steps as he had blundered through his speech. He tripped on the top step and steadied himself by grabbing Lucy's arm.

"Vote for me, Joe," she said, handing him one of her cards.

He tore off the taffy and popped it into his mouth.

"I'll vote for you, Lucy," he said, noisily sucking the candy, "if you'll promise to make a batch every week."

More students arrived. They came in twos and threes, and each ninth grader who passed took one of her cards. Not many promised to vote for her, but every one seemed pleased by the candy. The box was more than half empty when Tom walked up the steps.

Without a word of greeting he said, "Mabel's down at the corner. She'll be here any minute."

"Let her come," said Lucy. "She goes to school here, too." Mabel Smith was the last person in the world she wanted to see, but she pretended not to care.

Before Tom could reply, Mabel appeared at the bottom of the steps. She carried a dainty wicker basket trimmed with red satin ribbon. The morning sunlight glinted on the shiny pennies glued to the cards that filled the basket. Red ribbons trimmed Mabel's white ruffled dress, and another ribbon was perched on top of her yellow curls.

She walked slowly up the steps and stopped in a patch of sunshine just opposite Lucy. The two girls stood silently on each side of the door like soldiers on guard. Though Mabel said not a word, a look of surprise crossed her face when she saw the box in Lucy's hands.

A pair of boys walked up and took cards from the box and the basket.

"I guess Lucy's sweeter than Mabel," said one of the boys, laughing.

"But Mabel spends better," said the other. He looked at Tom, who stood behind Lucy. "Getting ideas for your own campaign?" he asked. "You'll have to go some to catch up with the girls."

Mr. Chester came up the steps, his long coat flapping around his legs and a stack of books under his arm. "Our two lady politicians," he said. He took a card from Mabel's basket and looked at it closely, then one from Lucy's. He shook his head. "A problem," he said, "hard candy or hard cash. I guess we can't solve that one with algebra." He smiled at his joke and trotted off into the building.

Only a few cards remained in the bottom of Lucy's box. She glanced across at Mabel. Mabel's dress was meant for a summer afternoon, and she shivered in the thin sunlight. From time to time she rubbed her shoulders, but spoke no word of complaint.

"It's too cold out here for me," said Lucy impulsively. As long as she stood on the steps, Mabel would stand there, too. "Let's go inside and get warm." She turned and walked up the steps, followed by Tom.

The door had no more than banged behind them before Mabel opened it and hurried inside. She swept past them without a word and turned down the corridor toward the classroom.

Lucy and Tom walked down the hall, toward the big bulletin board. In front of it stood a group of noisy students.

"Look!" said Tom. He steered Lucy toward the crowd.

In the center of the board, mounted on a large sheet of red paper, were two small white cards. Glued to one was a penny, to the other, a piece of taffy. Below them were two short lines in Mr. Chester's precise handwriting:

> Our female candidates are running hard,
> But where, oh where, are our hardy males?

"That's Mr. Chester's work," said Lucy. She sounded angry. "He making fun of you. I don't think that's fair."

"He should snoop around," said Tom. "He'd find that the males have been spending their time aiding the females. Do you see what would happen, Lucy, if women were given the vote? The men would all be so busy helping the ladies that they'd never get around to their own campaigns."

"And we'd have a woman mayor," said Lucy.

Tom laughed at the ridiculous idea. But Lucy only smiled. If a girl can run for class office, she thought, why can't a woman run for mayor? Or governor? Or even President? Tom would split his sides if she suggested that a woman might be in the White House one day. But why should the notion be so funny? She thought it was a good idea.

51

IX

WHEN LUCY WALKED into the dining room, Mother
was rubbing a silver fork with a piece of flannel. When
she held it to the light, it gleamed in the rays of the late
afternoon sun. Freshly polished silver covered the sideboard and the crystal candelabra stood on the best
damask tablecloth.

Lucy sensed trouble ahead. The good silver and the
crystal candlesticks came out of their wrappers only for
company. Yes, trouble loomed. With the house full of
guests, how would they ever get away to the park?

"Are we having company?" she asked.

Mother looked up from the gravy ladle. "Your father
has invited Mr. Harrison to supper," she said. "He
thought it would be nice for Letitia to meet a few gentlemen."

Jonathan Harrison owned the only department store in Smithville. He was a handsome, square-jawed man in his forties who never had married. Some people said it was because he never had the time. Every minute of his day was spent squeezing the last nickel and dime out of Harrison's Mercantile Company. He opened the store early each morning and worked late into the night after his employees had gone home. He was a deacon of the church, and each Sunday morning his rich baritone rang out from the last pew to overpower the struggling choir.

"What are we going to do?" asked Lucy. Her panic sounded through the words. "The meeting in the park begins at seven-thirty."

"We'll do the best we can," said Mother. "I'm sure that Mr. Harrison wouldn't want to stand in the way of choir practice. And we've already planned an early supper."

Lucy began to set the table. "What does Aunt Letitia think of her beau?" she asked.

"Your aunt doesn't even know he's coming. She went out again this afternoon without a word. I just hope she gets home in time to meet Mr. Harrison."

Each place was framed with its fork and knife and spoon. Lucy inspected the table and straightened a teaspoon that was out of line.

"What do you suppose Aunt Letitia does on her mysterious trips?" she asked. "She's been out every afternoon and some evenings, and she never says where she's gone or what she's done."

"I'm sure I don't know," said Mother. She returned the extra silver to the flannel cases and put them into the drawer. "At first I thought she was visiting old friends, but your father says she has no friends in Smithville."

The front door slammed and Aunt Letitia appeared. Lucy and Mother jumped like children caught with their hands in a cooky jar.

"Doesn't that table look nice," Letitia said. "Are you having a party?"

"Will has invited Jonathan Harrison for supper," said Mother. "He thought you might like to meet him."

Aunt Letitia made a face. "Another eligible bachelor, I suppose," she said. "People seem to feel they have to trot out every unmarried man they know when I come to visit. I should think they would have given up long ago."

She started for the stairs, her ugly black hat in her hand. "Don't count on me for the whole evening," she called. "I have to go out again at seven o'clock."

Mother and Lucy looked at each other. "Now what can we do?" wailed Lucy. "Somebody has to be polite to Mr. Harrison."

"Your father invited him," said Mother. "Let your father entertain him."

Lucy's spirits crept a little higher. When Mother's

voice took on what Father called her General Grant tone, she meant every word she said.

But a frown still wrinkled her forehead. And it was there while she helped Mother in the kitchen, and it was still there when they all sat down to eat.

Before Father took his seat at the head of the table, he placed Aunt Letitia at his right, next to Lucy, and Mr. Harrison across from her. Without waiting, Sam slid into his chair. While Father's back was turned, he reached for his glass of milk and drank half of it.

Father glanced at him. "How many times must I tell you, young man, that you are not to begin until after the blessing?" he said in a stern voice.

"What do you mean, sir?" asked Sam. His eyes were wide, but a white mustache on his upper lip betrayed him.

"Wipe the milk off your mouth and behave," said Father. "We have an important guest tonight."

Sam did as he was told. Then he folded his hands in his lap and looked down, waiting for Father to return thanks for the meal.

Father bowed his head and cleared his throat. Not even Sam dared look up as the nightly prayer began. "Bless this food to our use and our lives to Thy service, we ask in Jesus' name. Amen."

Before the Amen died away, Father began to fill the dinner plates. On each he put a thick slice of steaming meat loaf and a big baked potato that Mother had already opened and filled with butter. Beside the potato he placed a mound of sliced carrots and a spoonful of Mother's best corn relish.

For a time there was only the faint clatter of silver. Aunt Letitia and Mr. Harrison ate with their eyes cast down on their plates. Sam's interest was centered on his food, and he attacked it without looking to left or right.

Ordinarily Lucy would have been interested in her aunt and Mr. Harrison, but the trouble that lay between dinner and the meeting in the park loomed larger by the second. Father put aside his fork to butter a piece of Mother's freshly baked bread and glanced at her. "You seem upset, Lucy," he said. "Whatever is bothering you?"

She looked up at Father and then down at her plate. She swallowed and said quickly, "Nothing. Nothing at all."

"Something's wrong," he said. "That cloud on your face is there for some good reason."

"We have a history test tomorrow," said Lucy. "Miss Jefferson's tests are awfully hard. They would worry anyone."

"Never worried you much before," said Sam.

Lucy glared at her brother. "I was so busy this weekend that I didn't get to read one of the chapters," she said. Her glance fell on Sam's plate and she smiled.

"How do you expect to have curly hair if you hide your carrots under the potato skin?" she asked.

Both Father and Mother studied their son.

"If you expect any dessert, Sam, you'll have to eat your carrots," said Mother.

Father was more direct. "Eat your carrots!" he said.

Sam obeyed. He put a chunk of meat loaf on his fork, then a slice of carrot. He topped it all with a mound of potato and washed the sandwich down with a gulp of milk. After each bite he scowled at Lucy.

Mr. Harrison's throat rumbled several times. "Do you plan to stay long in Smithville, Miss Snow?" he asked.

Aunt Letitia raised her eyes from her meat loaf. "No more than a week," she replied. "I don't know if Will could put up with me much longer than that."

Mother and Father exchanged glances. Lucy was puzzled. If her aunt planned to leave in only a week, why had she brought three heavy trunks with her? A silence fell over the table as Sam and Mother and Father pondered the same point.

Suddenly Aunt Letitia's voice sounded loudly in the quiet room. "Relax, Mr. Harrison," she said. "You must get weary of being paraded for every visiting spinster."

Mr. Harrison flushed. "It . . . it's a pleasure to be asked to meet a lady," he stammered.

Quickly Father asked him if he had read an account

of President Roosevelt's latest speech. They began to talk politics. For the hundredth time the family learned how the country would be ruined if Judge Parker were elected President and what a great statesman Teddy Roosevelt was.

As he dutifully downed the last slice of carrot Sam said, "If Judge Parker is elected President, we'll have to go to school six days a week!"

"That's not true," said Aunt Letitia, sitting very straight in her chair. "Judge Parker would never make you go to school on Saturday."

"Well, well," said Father, "it appears we have a Democrat at our table."

Aunt Letitia peered at Father through her spectacles. "I'm neither a Republican nor a Democrat," she said, "but you shouldn't let the boy repeat such utter nonsense."

"Your aunt is right," said Father. "Judge Parker wouldn't think of making you go to school on Saturdays."

Sam blinked. His own father was defending a Democrat. "But you said Judge Parker would ruin the country. And if we had to go to school on Saturday, the country would sure be ruined."

"The President has nothing to say about school," Father replied. He shook his head at Sam's ignorance. "I'm sorry to see a son of mine so gullible as to believe such foolishness."

Mr. Harrison waved his fork at Sam. "When I was your age," he said, "the Democrats tried to tell me that Garfield would make us go to school on Saturday. Don't believe everything you hear."

"No, sir," Sam said meekly. "I won't."

As soon as dinner was over, Aunt Letitia and Lucy helped Mother clear the table and wash the dishes. They hurried, for it was already a quarter to seven. Soon the last fork was dried and every pot scoured.

Aunt Letitia put on her old black hat and picked up her umbrella. She opened the parlor door. The three women filed into the room.

"It was very nice to meet you," she said to Mr. Harrison.

Slowly he got to his feet. "Surely you're not leaving," he said. "The evening is still young."

"I'm already late for an engagement," she replied. "Goodbye, Mr. Harrison. Good night, Will." She nodded at both men and was gone.

"She can't do that," Father began.

Over the thud of the front door Mother broke in. "We're leaving now, dear."

"Leaving?" said Father. An odd look crossed his face as he realized that his wife and daughter were leaving him alone to entertain their guest.

"I'd forgotten that choir practice was tonight," he said.

"Choir practices every Thursday night," said Lucy.

Sam looked up from his arithmetic. "Why don't you

stay home?" he asked. "You're always running down to that church. The rest of them don't show up every week."

"When are you going to join the choir, Jonathan?" asked Father. "Seems to me that voice of yours belongs up front where the rest of us can enjoy it."

Mr. Harrison beamed and jingled the change in his vest pocket. "The preacher keeps after me to join," he said, "but I just don't have the time."

"Surprise him and show up tonight," said Father. "We certainly need some good strong voices down there. The choir overflows with sopranos."

Lucy bit her lip. She stared hard at Mr. Harrison and concentrated. Say no, she thought, say no, say no!

"Couldn't possibly," said Mr. Harrison.

Lucy relaxed and a smile broke over her face.

"I just can't get away from the business every Thursday night," Mr. Harrison explained. "And besides, there are just too darn many single ladies in that choir. They scare me. Always fluttering around a man until he can't breathe. Too bad there aren't more women like your sister."

Father was defeated. He reached into his vest pocket and pulled out his railroad watch. "You'd better run along now, ladies," he said. "It's a quarter after seven."

As they went down the path, Lucy found it hard to walk beside Mother. She wanted to skip and laugh and run. They were on their way and neither Father nor Sam suspected a thing. In just a few minutes they would see and hear the suffragist.

X

THE NIGHT WAS COLD. In the clear sky the stars glittered like tiny chunks of ice, and the full moon huddled for warmth in the outstretched limbs of an oak tree. A chill breeze nipped the leaves from the branches and sent them tumbling down the street.

Lucy and Mother drew their coats about them and hurried across the grass. A big crowd was gathered for the speech. But to Lucy's surprise, many boys and men were waiting to hear the program. Perhaps they had come because the suffragist on the posters was pretty, very pretty.

Her picture smiled down from nearly every tree in the park, but few in the crowd smiled back. The banners draped over the bandstand were gay and festive, but around the platform, the faces were serious — like

Mr. Amberson's when he came upon a student playing hooky.

Lucy peered ahead through the dark, trying to recognize the suffragist. She was so intent on picking out the speaker that she tripped over a root and stumbled.

"Be careful," said Mother. "If you sprain your ankle you won't hear a word of the speech."

They pushed into the crowd around the bandstand. Lucy searched the stage for the suffragist on the poster, but there was no dimpled, smiling, slender lady to be seen.

In the soft glow of gaslight, it was hard to make out the features of the three people who sat on the platform. On a straight, hard chair perched a small, frail man in a checkered suit. His hair was sparse and his nose was large; above his thin lips was a narrow mustache that looked as if it had been drawn with a crayon. Next to him sat a fat, smiling woman, who seemed incomplete without a small child at her knee, the kind of mother who solved all troubles with cookies and kisses.

Beside her, in a stiff-backed chair, sat the last person Lucy had expected to see. She rubbed her eyes and looked again. Surely there was some mistake. Perhaps this was not a rally for woman suffrage after all.

Just then the woman stood up, stepped out of the shadow, and walked to the front of the stage. Mother moaned, "Ye gods and little fishhooks! Your father will never get over this."

Lucy gulped. There was no mistake. The woman standing at the lectern, ready to speak, was Aunt Letitia.

In a quiet voice she greeted the crowd and thanked them for coming out on a frosty night. She said she had traveled all the way from New York to tell them about the woman suffrage movement.

Lucy clapped. And so did some of the others who stood before the platform. But Mother twisted her handkerchief, and there were boos and jeers and catcalls mixed with the applause.

Her aunt's soft voice changed. She began to speak in clear, ringing tones. She was neither timid nor frightened, but as sure as the Reverend Hinckley when he delivered his sermon on Sunday morning. She spoke of the way women were still bought and sold as slaves in Arab countries. She pointed out that while men said that the Bible called man superior to woman, they all must remember that the Bible had been written by men.

"If God had meant Eve to submit to man," she said, "He would have created her from Adam's leg or his foot. But Eve was taken from Adam's rib and was meant to be his equal, to stand by his side."

Snorts erupted from some of the men, but sighs of "Yes, yes," came from the women. Lucy glanced at Mother who, surprisingly, was nodding her head in agreement.

"In most of America women cannot vote," said Aunt Letitia, "yet in New Zealand and in Australia and in

Sweden women vote along with their men. Men say that women are weak . . ."

"You said it, sister," shouted a voice from the back of the crowd. "Weak as water."

"They say we are weak," she continued, as unruffled as if she were talking to her sewing circle, "but word comes this very day from South America that Miss Annie Peck has climbed Mount Sorata, a towering peak in the Andes. This frail woman has climbed nearer the top of that great forbidding mountain than any man has dared to go."

There was more laughter. This time it came from the women.

Aunt Letitia listed all the injustices suffered by females. She described what they had accomplished even under their oppressed condition. And as she talked, Lucy's excitement grew. For the first time she realized that women *were* oppressed. They were really nothing but slaves to the men who ran the world. She agreed that they should have the vote as the first step toward freedom. She would work and talk and do everything she could to help them reach that goal.

Since 1869, women had been voting in Wyoming, said Aunt Letitia, and they and the women of Colorado and Utah and Idaho would cast their ballots for President next month. And, she asked, why should a single one of those ballots be cast for Theodore Roosevelt or for Judge Parker?

A hush fell over the crowd. Not even a cough broke the stillness.

"Neither the Democrats nor the Republicans support woman suffrage," Aunt Letitia said. "Both parties refuse to extend simple justice to females. But there are two parties who back the right of women to vote. Women in four states will flock to their banners. They will vote the Prohibition and the Socialist tickets."

Loud hisses came from all parts of the crowd.

"Go back to the kitchen," shouted a deep voice.

When the noise died down, Aunt Letitia went on. "President Roosevelt is no friend of woman suffrage," she said. "He told Susan B. Anthony that 'it wasn't very important.'"

Shocked sighs from women mingled with manly cries of "You bet!"

"What is more," said Aunt Letitia, "President Roosevelt has no use for higher education for women. He has denied college educations to his own daughters."

"How dare he!" an indignant voice broke in.

Lucy jumped. The voice was beside her. It belonged to her mother.

From far back in the crowd a small object sailed over Lucy's head and smashed upon the platform. The stench of a rotten egg filled the air. Then a second egg crashed on the stage. And yet another. Aunt Letitia stopped speaking.

With dismay Lucy watched eggs splatter on the chairs,

on the wooden floor and on the smiling posters. Suddenly she realized that the men of Smithville had never intended to let her aunt speak. Those same men who claimed that women needed protection had come to the park with plans to humiliate a lone woman.

Lucy became angry. It was unjust. How dare they treat her aunt like that. She faced the crowd and shouted, "Let her alone. She has a right to speak."

Shouts drowned her voice. Her heart began to pound. Someone must help Aunt Letitia. She took a step toward the platform.

Then an egg broke against her aunt's shoulder and the yolk dripped down her dress. With her head held high, she turned and walked off the platform.

"Look at that old crowing hen run for cover," someone gleefully shouted.

A hail of eggs followed Aunt Letitia until she disappeared behind the bandstand. But Lucy had no chance to see where her aunt went next.

A sharp cracking noise made her jump to the side. Above her head a limb split and dry leaves rustled as a small figure plunged through the air and landed with a thump at her feet.

The boy untangled himself from the broken branch, sat up and looked around. "Jeehosophat!" he said. "I thought you were at choir practice."

"Samuel Snow, just what do you think you're doing?" shouted Lucy.

Sam rubbed his head and blinked. His face was white, even in the faint light around the bandstand. He looked from Mother to Lucy and swallowed hard.

"How did you get out of the house, Samuel?" asked Mother. Her voice was the one she used when Sam spent his Sunday school money for candy.

"I . . ." Sam began. He stopped, then started again. "I told Father I was sleepy and went upstairs to my room. Then I climbed out my window and slid down the drainpipe." He kicked at the ground with his toe. Then he looked up and his eyes widened. "But Father thinks you're at choir practice," he said.

Suddenly there were three conspirators where there had been only two. No one spoke.

At last Mother sighed. "Samuel," she said in a voice that no longer threatened, "we're going to walk home now. When we get back to the house, I shall expect to find you in your bed, sound asleep. And we shall be so tired that we'll be upstairs immediately."

A grin broke across Sam's face. "Yes, ma'am," he said. He started for home as fast as he could.

Lucy watched him disappear among the trees. He would keep their secret to save his own hide. But what if Father looked in Sam's room before he got home? What if Sam were caught climbing into his window? She suddenly realized that it didn't really matter. All she had heard tonight seemed so important that Father's disapproval no longer frightened her.

"I guess Father will find out we were here," she said.

Mother shook her head. "Don't worry about it," she said. "When he hears that your Aunt Letitia was the speaker, it really won't make much difference. Just be prepared for a grand explosion."

They set off for home through the nearly deserted park. The men and boys had melted away as soon as their target disappeared. The women left more slowly, stopping in little groups to talk in agitated whispers.

Smithville would never be the same again.

XI

Lucy stopped talking in the middle of a word, but Mother did not notice. The glow of the porchlight could not chase the gloom that settled over them when they turned the corner and saw the house standing ghostlike before them.

Mother repeated her instructions for the third time. "I'll keep Father busy in the parlor while you wait up to help your aunt," she said. "He'll find out what happened soon enough, and there's no point in starting a big ruckus tonight."

They tiptoed through the gate and up the steps. Carefully Mother opened the front door. Lucy hurried to the stairs and began to climb to the second floor. As she reached the landing, she could hear Father's voice boom from the parlor, "And did you shake the church rafters with your singing?"

Lucy scurried into her room and closed the door. She leaned against it and listened, opened it a crack.

Father's voice floated up the stairs. "Just a touch of cheese on that pie."

It was safe. She tiptoed down the corridor. After a short wait she knocked on a closed door. Three sharp raps, a pause, then three more raps.

"Come in," said a muffled voice.

As the door swung open, the faint creak of the hinges sounded like a scream. She closed the door, crept over to the bed and asked softly, "Did Father catch you?"

A red head appeared from beneath the covers. "Heck no," Sam whispered. "I skinned up that drainpipe like a cat. Father never once took his nose out of the newspaper."

He sat up in bed. "How did you ever talk Mother into taking you to the park?"

Lucy smiled mysteriously. "There are ways," she said in her most superior voice. "Some people don't have to sneak out of windows. Some people can walk out the front door in a proper, genteel manner."

Sam mocked her tone. "And some people who walk out in a proper, genteel manner are scared to death their fathers will find out where they walked."

Lucy's smile faded. Sam always found her weak spot. "I just wanted to be sure everything was all right," she said. "I'll go back to my room now."

She was on her way out the door when her glance fell on a stack of papers that lay on Sam's dresser. She picked up the top sheet. "Help women get the vote" said the letters at the top of the page. The handbill urged each citizen to write his representatives and say that women deserved the right to vote. It listed the addresses of the President, the governor, senators, congressmen and state legislators.

"Where did you get these?" asked Lucy, an idea beginning to take shape.

"You'll never guess," Sam said. "My window was stuck, so I climbed into Aunt Letitia's room. One of her big trunks was open and I looked inside to see what made it so heavy." His voice became hushed. "It's full of paper!" he said. "Clear to the brim. I'll bet there are millions of those handbills in her trunks."

Lucy chewed on her thumb. The idea grew clearer.

"Do you suppose she's crazy?" asked Sam.

"Don't be silly," said Lucy. "What are you going to do with the handbills?"

"I don't know. It just seemed like a good idea to pick them up." Sam's eyes twinkled. "Maybe Father would like to add one to each delivery he makes tomorrow."

"Very funny," said Lucy. Then her voice became earnest. "Give them to me."

Sam became wary. "What for?"

"Oh, I'd just like to have them," said Lucy, as if the handbills were of no more interest than the label on a pickle jar.

"No." Sam shook his head. "Why should I give them to you? They're mine."

Lucy was determined. "Give them to me or I'll tell Father you sneaked out tonight."

"And how will you tell him you found out?" asked Sam confidently. "You were in the park, too, Miss Smarty. And so was Aunt Letitia."

Lucy played her trump card. "But I was with Mother," she said. "I won't get punished."

"Go ahead," said Sam, "see if I care." He lay down and pulled the covers up to his chin.

"All right," said Lucy, "you had your chance." She marched to the door and reached for the knob.

"Oh, take your old handbills," called Sam. He turned toward the wall and pulled the blanket over his head. "What can you do with those old things?" he muttered, his voice muffled by the bedclothes.

Lucy smiled and picked up the stack of leaflets. She carried them down the hall and tucked them under her petticoats in the bureau drawer.

As soon as she could, she would give them away. She sat on the edge of the bed and took off her shoes and stockings. She stared into space, one shoe clutched in her hand. Yes, Aunt Letitia was right. She would help in any way she could. And the first thing to do was to put one of those leaflets into every hand in Smithville.

The sound of footsteps broke into her thoughts. She ran to the door and opened it a crack. With a rustle of skirts, her aunt hurried down the hall to the back bedroom. Lucy followed, her bare feet making no sound on the polished wooden floor.

Aunt Letitia slipped inside her room. Before she could turn the latch, Lucy knocked softly on the door. It opened just wide enough for her aunt to peer out.

"What is it, child?" she asked in a tone that clearly said, go away and don't bother me.

"Can I help?" asked Lucy. "Do you need water to sponge the egg off your dress? Is there anything I can get you?"

The door swung open. "Come in," said her aunt. "Does Will know what went on tonight?"

Lucy stepped inside. "Father hasn't heard," she said. "Mother and Sam and I were in the park. But we didn't know you would be the speaker."

She looked at Aunt Letitia. The ugly black hat was missing. Wisps of hair hung over her forehead. Her spectacles dangled from one ear. Yellow splotches of yolk smeared her skirt and shoulder. And she had lost her umbrella.

"There's water in the pitcher," said Aunt Letitia. "But if you can get me something for a headache, I'd appreciate it."

Lucy hurried down the hall to her parents' room. She found Father's headache powders and took one packet from the box. As she passed the stairs on her way back, she could hear quiet voices in the parlor. It was still safe.

Aunt Letitia emptied the white powder into a glass of water. It foamed and bubbled, making noises that echoed in the quiet room. She drained the glass and set it on the bureau.

"There!" she said. "I'll feel better soon, I hope."

She took off her spectacles and unbuttoned her dress. Lucy helped her pull the long, full skirts over her head. She stood watching as her aunt took the pins from her hair and it fell in soft waves over her shoulders.

"Now we're ready to get to work," Letitia said.

Lucy stood as if mesmerized. In her red ruffled petticoat, with her glasses off and her hair down, Aunt Letitia looked very much like the girl in the photograph. The piercing look was gone from her eyes, and her hard features seemed soft and feminine.

Suddenly Lucy became aware of her aunt's outstretched hand. She started and then handed her the dress. Aunt Letitia spread it on the bed and shook her head.

"It looks as if I ran into a bucket of yellow paint," she said.

Lucy poured water into the basin. Dipping their cloths, they each began to sponge a section of the dress.

75

For a time they worked in silence. Lucy had never been alone with her aunt before, and she was not used to thinking of Aunt Letitia as a crusader.

"Whatever possessed you to come to the park tonight?" asked her aunt.

"I wanted to see a real suffragist," said Lucy. She smiled shyly. "I didn't know there was one right here in the house. "

"I thought it wise to say nothing to Will until I had to," said Aunt Letitia. "He'll find out soon enough." She stopped daubing at her dress and looked at Lucy. "Now that you've seen your suffragist, what do you think?"

"I think you're very brave," said Lucy. "And I think women should have the vote. And I think men are unfair."

"Good for you," said Aunt Letitia. "If everyone felt that way, the battle would be won." She patted Lucy's hand. "You remind me of myself at your age," she said. "My hair was just the color of yours, my tongue was always getting me into trouble, and I had a little brother, too." She grew quiet.

Lucy sponged the last of the egg off the black skirt. She hesitated. If Aunt Letitia were ever to tell why she left Smithville, now was the time. "Why did you go to New York?" she asked.

"You mean Will has never told you?"

"He just gets red in the face and says that it wouldn't interest me."

"He's worse than I thought," said Aunt Letitia. She hung the damp dress on the cupboard door. "Poor Will! There's no reason why you shouldn't know. When I was eighteen, I went for a buggy ride with a young man. We were alone and it was a warm summer night, perfect for a drive in the country. The time slipped away and it was quite late when we turned the horse around and started back."

Aunt Letitia's voice became dreamy, as if she were talking to herself. "I knew Father would be upset so I asked Henry to drive faster. The old horse began to gallop and on one of the bends in the road the buggy slipped off the path. I guess it must have hit a rock. Something broke a wheel and we were stranded — five miles from town. My skirts were tangled and I turned my ankle getting down from the seat. It was swollen and hurt so that I couldn't walk. There we were — all night. Next morning about daylight a farmer picked us up and took us home in his wagon. Two years later I left Smithville."

She picked up a hairbrush and began to brush her hair.

Lucy frowned. "I don't understand," she said. "What did the buggy ride have to do with your leaving Smithville?"

A long sigh came from Aunt Letitia. She placed the brush on the dresser and turned to face Lucy.

"No one in Smithville would let me forget that night in the country," she said. "Two years later I was still that awful girl who stayed out with a man until morning. I couldn't stand it, so I left for New York where it wouldn't matter."

"What happened to the young man?" asked Lucy.

Her aunt laughed. "We never had another buggy ride. After all, my reputation had been ruined. But young men can't be compromised. Henry Clark still lives in Smithville."

Lucy's eyes widened. "You mean Judge Clark?"

"Yes. He was judging people even then," said Aunt Letitia. "I guess after all these years I had to come back to prove something to myself. Tonight's program could have been held anywhere, but I had to give that speech here in Smithville." She paused. "I suppose you could say that night with Henry Clark was the making of a suffragist. Twenty-five years ago I thought men and women should be treated the same, and I still think that way."

"So do I," said Lucy. "So do I. And I want to work for women's rights. I'm going to do everything I can to help the cause."

"Be sure before you begin," said Aunt Letitia. "It's not a tea party, and your mother won't be there to hold your hand. They'll throw eggs at you — and rocks.

I've been insulted by rowdies. I've been cursed by gentlemen. I've been arrested. Once I chained myself to a ballot box and was there for five hours before they sawed through the steel links with a hacksaw."

There was no answer from Lucy. She was lost in a dream. She saw herself stand bravely before a mob of shouting roughnecks, not flinching under the shower of eggs that rained from all sides. She would be another Joan of Arc.

"What happens when your father finds out?" asked her aunt. "He will, you know."

Joan of Arc melted before the vision of her outraged father. "I know," said Lucy slowly, "but I want to vote someday. And that's a chance I'll take."

XII

Breakfast was peaceful. Father joked with Aunt
Letitia, observing that Mr. Harrison was madly in love
with her. Aunt Letitia kept on buttering her toast and
replied that if he fell in love that easily, he was an utter
fool. Lucy told Mother about the election placards she
and Tom would hang in the school corridors that day.
Sam said not a word. He kept his eyes on his bowl of
oatmeal as though he expected a pearl among the raisins
in his next spoonful. No one mentioned the speech in
the park.

That morning in every corner of the school yard the
eggs that splattered on the platform and on Aunt Letitia's dress were thrown in memory again and again.
With each telling the number grew. By noon, the tale

had become an account of a battle in which the towns-men, armed only with a basket of rotten eggs, bravely routed a battalion of umbrella-wielding harridans.

At a quarter after twelve, when Lucy walked through the front door at home, she could hear Father's angry voice. As she neared the kitchen, she could sort out the words.

"How dare they start a commotion in our town?" Father was nearly shouting. He followed Mother as she walked from the kitchen to the dining room and back again. Even the platter of fried steak she set on the table did not loosen the fingers that suddenly gripped Lucy's stomach.

"It's bad enough," Father said, "that these unnatural females came into Smithville." He shook his fist. "But when they start a fight in the park, they have lost all right to respect."

Aunt Letitia said nothing. She began to slice the bread, and Father stood just behind her. Lucy held her breath. Each time her aunt drew the knife through the loaf, it looked as if her elbow would jab Father in the stomach.

Did Father know that Aunt Letitia was the speaker? Lucy glanced at her aunt, but Letitia's face told her nothing. No, she decided, listening to Father's words, he had no idea of his family's whereabouts last night.

Her lips set in a grim line, her head erect, the plate of bread held before her, Aunt Letitia marched into the dining room. Mother followed, carrying a bowl of steaming gravy, while Father, close at her heels, talked on and on about the riot in the park.

"I think we're ready to eat," said Mother, just as Sam clattered up the steps and banged open the front door.

He pulled out his chair, but before he could sit down, Mother spoke.

"Go and wash your hands, young man," she said.

Lucy followed Sam into the kitchen. He turned on the tap and passed his fingers gingerly through the cold water.

"Be careful," said Lucy. "You'll get wet."

Sam ignored her and reached for a towel. "What's Father making such a fuss about?" he asked.

"He's upset about the ruckus last night. But he still doesn't know about Aunt Letitia — or us."

"When he finds out," said Sam, "then he will yell." He leaned against the wooden sink board. "Don't let on."

Lucy's smile hid an inside like jelly. "Scared, little boy?" she asked.

"Sure," said Sam. "And don't tell me you're not scared, too. You're not that dumb." He tossed the towel to Lucy.

Thoughtfully she dried her hands. Father, she was certain, would discover that Aunt Letitia was the woman who had caused the fight in the park. And if he should ask, Mother would confess everything. Horrible scenes flashed through Lucy's head. She saw herself driven from home in a blinding snowstorm. She heard Father say, "No daughter of mine will ever be a wicked suffragette." But the day was clear and even a little warm for October.

Father's voice boomed from the dining room. Lucy jumped, before she realized that he had said only, "We're waiting dinner for you, young lady."

With her spine stiff, Lucy marched in, feeling like an early Christian walking into the jaws of the lions waiting in the Colosseum.

But things were calm during the meal. Mother's fried steak and potatoes seemed to sooth Father's anger. And Sam was very careful to say nothing that would remind him of the park. Aunt Letitia talked easily about the election, asking Lucy if she had hung all her posters.

It was only after dinner that the sky fell in. Sam had gone back to school to play baseball before class. Lucy sat in the window seat, glancing idly at the *Ladies' Home Journal*. Aunt Letitia's knitting needles clicked busily, and Mother sorted the scraps of material that spilled over the edges of a large box.

"What are you doing there, Maud?" asked Father. He sat in his big leather chair, resting before he went back to his afternoon's work on the dray.

"I'm looking for material that would make doll clothes or stuffed toys or baby dresses. The Sewing Circle has taken the Donovan family as their Christmas project. We'll fix a Christmas basket and make new clothes and toys for all the children."

"It's hard to raise seven children without a man in the house," said Father.

"And it's harder to live on the charity of your neighbors," said Mother. She held up a length of white cloth sprigged with tiny pink rosebuds. "Mrs. Donovan can't make ends meet."

"It was generous of the railroad to give her a pension," said Father. "It's been nearly a year since Charlie Donovan was killed and she still gets a check every month."

Aunt Letitia looked up from her knitting. "It would have been better for Charlie Donovan if the railroad equipment had been in good condition," she said. "Then those seven children would still have a father."

"Now, now, Letitia," said Father. "The railroad didn't have to give the Donovans a dime."

The magazine slid unnoticed from Lucy's lap.

"A dime describes it," said Mother. "That pension hardly keeps the family alive." She folded the material and put it aside.

"If women arranged things," said Aunt Letitia, "there would be laws to make jobs like Charlie's safer. And a widow would get a respectable pension."

Father frowned. "You're beginning to sound like a

Socialist," he said. "A Socialist suffragette."

"At least the Socialists would allow women to vote," said Aunt Letitia. Her cheeks glowed pink.

Father's feet came off the hassock with a jerk. "You must be out of your head, Letitia." He struggled to control himself. "I know you don't mean to talk like a suffragette."

Lucy looked from Aunt Letitia to Father and waited for the next word.

"There's no reason why I shouldn't talk like one," said her aunt. "I was the woman, the unnatural female who spoke in the park last night."

Father's mouth opened and closed like a goldfish. "My own sister!" he sputtered. "And under my very roof!" He sank back in his chair, unable to say a word. He looked wildly about the room. His glance finally fell on Lucy.

"Next you'll be making a suffragette out of my own daughter," he said in a strained voice. "And she'll be running around at night in the park, getting insulted, dodging rocks and rotten eggs."

Lucy wished the window seat would fly open and let her drop inside. But she knew the moment had come to make a stand.

"I've already been in the park at night," she said. "I heard Aunt Letitia speak and I intend to do everything I can to help women get the vote."

"Did you hear that, Maud?" shouted Father. "Your own daughter was out gallivanting with those shameless suffragettes."

"Yes, I know," said Mother, as if she were saying, 'please pass the butter.' She folded a square of bright, red print and looked up at Father. "I know because I was with her."

Father clutched at his hair. "Is nothing sacred?" he asked. He whirled toward Aunt Letitia and pointed a shaking finger at her. "You come into my house and persuade my wife and my daughter to violate my wishes. You tend to your knitting and leave my family alone. Flesh and blood go only so far."

Lucy swallowed hard. She had to defend her aunt. "It's not Aunt Letitia's fault," she said. "It was my idea to go. I begged Mother to take me. I wanted to see a suffragist. I didn't know it was Aunt Letitia."

Father just stared at her.

"But the suffragists didn't riot," she said. The words came out in a croak. "Aunt Letitia was brave. It was the men and boys. They threw the rotten eggs."

"How sharper than a serpent's tooth," said Father, "it is to have a thankless child."

Lucy waited for a lecture. But Father looked at Mother, who gazed back at him steadily.

"I want no more of this, Lucy," he said quietly. "You confine your politics to that school election." He stood up and strode out of the room.

The front door slammed, and Lucy watched him walk out to the dray and the waiting horses.

Aunt Letitia took off her spectacles and wiped her eyes. "Will always did have a temper," she said.

Mother smiled at Lucy. "It'll be all right," she said. "He'll get over it."

Lucy smiled back, but just with her lips. Now Father had forbidden her to have anything to do with suffragists. Never had she disobeyed his direct orders, but she could not desert the cause of woman suffrage.

XIII

Sunlight wakened Lucy from a restless sleep. In her dreams, she had run down the streets of a strange city, chased by Father and Sam, who shouted and pelted her with rotten eggs. Mr. Chester stepped into her path, a nightcap on his head and his long side hair down around his shoulders. As she ran by, he tapped the pavement with his long pointer and asked for the square root of nine crowing hens. She rounded a corner and ran into three ugly witches who charged her with big, black umbrellas.

Just at this moment, Lucy rubbed her eyes and sat up in bed. Slowly she realized that she would be late for school. Then she happily remembered it was Saturday.

She snuggled back under the covers, waiting for the

smell of coffee and bacon to drift up the stairs and tell her it was time for breakfast. As she drowsed, her half-closed eyes fell upon the stack of papers that lay on her dresser. At once her eyes flew open, she jumped out of bed and began to pull on her clothes.

Last night she had taken the handbills from beneath her petticoats in the bureau drawer and put them where she would see them first thing in the morning. She planned to spread the leaflets from one end of Smith-ville to the other. But she was not going to discuss her project at the breakfast table. Not even Aunt Letitia would know.

As soon as the dishes were washed, Lucy put on her warmest sweater and mittens and left the house. The frost-covered grass sparkled as the sun began to melt the ice. She ran down the steps and turned up the sidewalk just in time to meet the postman on his morning rounds.

He looked up from a stack of letters that fluttered in the wind and smiled. "Good morning, Lucy," he said.

"Good morning, Mr. Bradley," Lucy called over her shoulder.

She hurried along through the copper and gold leaves that were scattered over the ground. Not until she reached the corner did it occur to her that she had not given Mr. Bradley a leaflet.

Just as she reached the Bryans', Tom came around the corner of the house and called to her. She stopped and waited for him to cross the yard.

"What are you up to this morning?" he asked. "You look as if you're on your way to a fire."

Without a word Lucy handed the leaflets to him.

Tom tucked his rake under one arm and read the top paper. He whistled. "Help women get the vote," he said. "You really meant it when you said that a woman should be President." He gave her the stack of papers and leaned on his rake.

"Of course I did," said Lucy. "It's not fair that only men can vote and hold office. If I can be secretary of the ninth grade, why can't I be mayor of Smithville?"

"Perhaps because you're not old enough," said Tom with a laugh. "I can hear it now, 'Ask Madame Mayor if her father will allow her to attend tonight's council meeting.'"

"Oh, Tom," said Lucy. She tossed her head. "Be serious. You know what I mean. Why can't my mother be mayor?"

"Because your father would have apoplexy," said Tom. "You're silly, Lucy. You know most women are only interested in their homes and that sort of thing."

"You're just like all men," said Lucy. "Because some women don't want to be mayor, why should all of them be forbidden to run for office?"

"Because . . ." Tom began. Then he stopped and scratched his head. He looked at Lucy for a long time. "Darned if I know why," he said.

Lucy's smile spread from ear to ear. "Then you're

for woman suffrage. I knew you were smart, Tom. Will you help me pass out these leaflets?"

Tom backed away. "Now just a minute, Lucy. It's all right with me if women vote — as long as my mother doesn't get mixed up in it. And as long as my wife stays home and minds her business." He shook the lawn rake. "Besides, I have to get these leaves raked before ten o'clock."

"If that's the way you feel, you'll have a hard time ever finding a wife," said Lucy. Without looking at him, she tucked the leaflets under her arm and straightened her mittens. "I certainly don't know anyone who would want the job," she added.

"I give up," Tom said. "Come back at ten o'clock and I'll help you." His face suddenly grew serious. "Be careful where you go with those leaflets," he said. "Some fool might throw a rock instead of an egg."

"I'll be back at ten," said Lucy. As she hurried down the street, Tom began to rake the yard with long, thoughtful strokes. At times he shook his head.

Lucy met several people in the next block, but in each case she found a reason to pass them without a word. One looked cross, another was too rushed to be stopped, a third had his arms loaded with packages. This would never do. She would show Tom she could get rid of every leaflet. She resolved to give a handbill to the next person she saw, no matter who it was.

She crossed the street and stepped up on the curb.

Just then a door down the block opened and a man walked out of the house and along the path. He was wrapped in an overcoat, a hat was pulled low over his face and his hands were thrust deep into his pockets.

Lucy gripped the stack of leaflets and rehearsed just what she would say. When he was still two houses away, he raised his head and looked directly at her.

Lucy stopped in the middle of a step. Swallowing hard, she looked from side to side like a rabbit searching for a hole. Of all the citizens of Smithville, why did the first one have to be a man with a round nose, shaggy eyebrows and baggy pants — the high school principal, Mr. Amberson!

"Mr. Amberson," she began with a croak. Clearing her throat, she tried again. "Good morning, Mr. Amberson."

The Santa Claus face broke into a smile. "Why, good morning, Lucy," he said. The dark eyes under the beetling brows were friendly. "Not giving any speeches this morning, are you?"

"Not . . . not exactly," said Lucy slowly. With a trembling hand she thrust out the leaflet. All the slogans she had planned, all the clever golden words slipped away. She stood there speechless, smiling weakly, waiting for Mr. Amberson to accept the paper she held toward him.

He took the leaflet and held it close to his eyes, then fumbled inside his coat. He hooked a pair of gold-rimmed spectacles over his ears. "Now let's see what we have here," he said. As he read the words printed in black letters, the smile left his face and the twinkle vanished from his eye. "What's this?" he snorted. "Votes for women? Women in politics. Where did you get this twaddle?"

Lucy stepped back. "From . . . from my brother," she said in a small voice.

Mr. Amberson scowled. "I'll warrant your father doesn't know what you're up to," he said. "And I don't think you do either. You're a pretty girl, Lucy. A very pretty girl. It's a pleasure to watch those green eyes sparkle and look at that glossy red hair.

"And what will happen to you if you keep up this kind of nonsense? Your voice will be shrill and you'll wind up on a platform somewhere — a spinster shrieking at a mob and getting pelted by rotten eggs in return."

"I don't care how many eggs they throw," said Lucy. "And I'm the same person, whether I stay at home or speak out for women."

The principal shook his head. "Look at your aunt. She was every bit as pretty as you. She could still be pretty, if she'd only put her mind to womanly things. But no, she's out antagonizing every man within shouting distance."

The scowl left Mr. Amberson's face and he sounded tired. "You'll turn bitter, Lucy. And you'll get lines in

93

your face and gray in your hair. And what will you have to show for it? Just grief."

He placed his hand on her shoulder and smiled. "Put this foolishness behind you. Suffrage is too complicated for so young a head. Your mother's a charming woman, with a lovely home and a fine family. If you want to be like her, go back to your games and leave politics to your elders." He put the leaflet gently into her hand and walked away.

Back to her games, indeed. That was exactly what was wrong. Too many women were content with their games when they should be concerned with their rights.

The more she thought about Mr. Amberson's words, the angrier she became. She began to walk without noticing which way she was going. Not once did she pause to hand out a leaflet. Too complicated for so young a head, was it?

She turned the corner. The flapping of paper caught her eye. Torn loose, a suffragist poster fluttered in the wind. Someone had drawn a fierce black mustache on the smiling face. If she went back to her games, all traces of her aunt's visit would soon disappear.

XIV

Lucy LOOKED AROUND and realized that she was only a block away from Mr. Johnson's grocery, where everyone in town stopped on Saturday morning. She walked briskly down the road and turned into Main Street.

There, on the covered walk, Mr. Johnson had set crates of carrots and parsnips and turnips and cabbages. Burlap sacks full of potatoes and onions lay on either side of the door. Fat pumpkins were stacked in clumsy pyramids. From inside the store, the smell of coffee beans and licorice and tea and spices drifted into the street.

Lucy took a deep breath. It always smelled so good at the store. She closed her eyes and sniffed again. If coffee only tasted as good as it smelled.

At the sound of footsteps she looked up to see Mrs. Rasmussen walking toward the store. She stood very straight and when Mrs. Rasmussen reached the door, she stepped forward and gave her one of the leaflets.

"Good morning," said Mrs. Rasmussen. She glanced at the paper and put it inside her pocketbook. "Good for you. It's time women had a say in these things. But don't give one to Mr. Rasmussen. He thinks women belong in the kitchen." She went inside and Lucy heard her ask Mr. Johnson for a pound of butter.

Not everyone was as friendly as Mrs. Rasmussen. At least half the women she met were not pleased. Some refused to take the leaflets or else they dropped them on the ground. But many handbills were carefully tucked into pockets and shopping bags.

The leaflets were nearly gone when Mabel Smith's mother came up the walk. When Lucy held out a leaflet, Mrs. Smith stopped. She let go of her skirt, which she had been holding away from the dirt of the road.

"What have we here?" she asked, glancing at the handbill. Her cool voice became sharp and she whirled on Lucy. "Just what do you mean by passing out this radical trash?"

Lucy gulped. "Wouldn't you like to vote for Teddy Roosevelt?" she asked.

"My husband will vote for President Roosevelt, thank you," said Mrs. Smith, "if it's any business of yours." She shook the leaflet at Lucy. "You shouldn't be permitted to distribute this garbage in the streets of Smith-ville."

She inspected Lucy. "You're Will Snow's daughter? Of course you are. I'll bet he doesn't know what you're up to." Her eyes narrowed. "And you're running against Mabel for class secretary. Oh, she's told me about you. It will be a sad day for Smithville High if you manage to win. Slipping around with your radical ideas, poisoning the minds of our fine young girls."

All at once it seemed as if the cold eyes and the angry, imperious voice belonged to Mabel Smith. Lucy had never realized how closely the daughter resembled her mother. The school election became more important than ever. She just had to defeat Mabel.

"But, Mrs. Smith," she said, "if it's all right for Mabel to run for class secretary, why is it so wrong to give her the right to run for Congress?"

Mrs. Smith blinked. "It's useless to talk to people like you." With a swish of her skirts, she flounced away. But a loud ripping sound stopped her before she reached the door. Her black taffeta dress had caught on a wooden crate. A ruffled petticoat showed through a long ragged tear. Mrs. Smith bent down and unhooked her skirt. She glared at Lucy, as if the box had acted on Lucy's orders.

She had never seen a human being so angry. Mrs. Smith would probably tell Father — if Mr. Amberson didn't tell him first. That bird on her hat should be a vulture, not a dove. Her weak laughter suddenly stopped when Mr. Johnson appeared in the door of the grocery store.

He wiped his hands on his long, white apron. "All right, Lucy," he said in a tired voice, "move away from the front of the store. And take those leaflets with you."

She looked him squarely in the eye. "I'm not hurting anything," she said.

"You've offended one of my best customers," he said. He adjusted the elastic band that kept up the sleeve of his striped shirt. "I can't afford to let you stand around here any longer. I'm sorry." He picked up two bunches of parsnips and carried them back into the store.

Lucy counted the leaflets. Only six left. She could give those out as she walked home. Before she had taken more than a few steps, she heard the clop-clop of horses' hoofs and the rattle of boxes, followed by a shout. The familiar sounds made her jump. Quickly she thrust the leaflets inside her sweater and buttoned it up to her chin. She waited as Father pulled the dray to a stop beside her.

He took off his hat with a flourish. "Would you like a lift, young lady?" he asked. "I'm on my way to Harrison's Mercantile with a load from the nine-fifteen."

Lucy stepped off the curb and patted Sinner, the big black gelding. "No, thank you, Father," she said, stroking the horse's neck. The leaflets inside her sweater crackled sharply. She drew back. If Father spied them there would be trouble. She spoke carefully. "I'm on my way home now."

Just then Saint, who looked like a Sinner dipped in whitewash, gave a loud whinny. Father reached into his pocket and pulled out a piece of carrot. He held it toward Lucy.

"You'd better give this to Saint," he said. "He's jealous."

She held the carrot up to Saint's mouth. The big white horse drew back his lips and delicately took the treat from her open palm.

"It's not fair, Father," she said. "Sinner should have a carrot, too." Sinner rubbed his head along her arm as if he understood her words. The leaflets rustled again, but only Lucy appeared to hear the noise.

"I knew you'd stick up for that black devil," said Father. "But I don't seem to have any more carrot." He searched his pockets. Sinner shook his head and the harness jingled.

"Listen to him ask for his share," said Father. "Next thing I know, you'll be teaching him to talk." He produced a piece of carrot.

Lucy took it and fed Sinner. "He knows you would not run out of treats so early in the day," she said.

"Well, I must be on my way," said Father. He picked up the reins. "Can't keep the customers at Harrison's waiting all day for the latest goods from New York."

She waved as Father shook the reins and clicked his tongue at the horses. Saint and Sinner lifted their hoofs high, and the shiny red dray rolled down the street.

XV

THE SUN SHONE BRAVELY. The wind that knifed
through the heaviest coat died down. The frost melted,
even in the shady corners.

Smoke from burning leaves stung Lucy's nose. The
smell of autumn bonfires always reminded her of the
times she had jumped into the piles of oak and maple
leaves that Father raked together. But that was two or
three years ago, when she was small.

Last year she had rolled in the leaves only once. Before she could brush the dry leaves from her skirt and
hair, Mother stood on the front porch. She called Lucy
indoors and gave her a long lecture on what young
ladies did and did not do.

They did not roll in leaves. They did not climb
trees. They did not ride horses bareback, their long legs

dangling on each side of the horse and their skirts hiked up about their waists. In short, young ladies did none of the things Lucy liked most to do. Sometimes she thought women had no fun at all. And once they were married, they might as well be dead.

She turned the corner and there was Tom, his back to her, leaning on his rake and staring into a pile of smoldering leaves. White smoke trailed up into the sky, but there was no flame to be seen.

"Why don't you let the leaves dry out before you burn them?" she asked.

Tom started at the sound of her voice, then smiled. "Hi, Lucy," he said. "I didn't hear you sneak up on me." He stirred the fire with the end of his rake. "The wind might scatter them again, and Pa said he'd skin me if he found a single leaf in the front yard tonight."

"Maybe an old newspaper would help them burn," said Lucy. "We wouldn't want the next treasurer to run around without his skin."

He leaned the rake against a tree. "You still want to play politician?" he asked.

"Oh, I'm all finished," said Lucy. She showed him her empty hands.

"I'd hoped you would save one for . . ." Tom paused when shouts and the sounds of blows filled the air.

He ran toward the noise and Lucy followed as fast as her skirts would let her. As they rounded the corner, they came upon half a dozen boys engaged in fierce combat. Scattered over the sidewalk were pieces of chalk, some of them ground into white powder by the shoes of the fighters.

Sitting astride another boy and punching him methodically was a familiar figure. Each time he hit his adversary, he demanded, "Say uncle." The boy who lay on his back thrashed violently, trying to kick his assailant.

"Sam Snow!" shrieked Lucy. She turned to Tom, who was watching the fight with his arms folded. "Can't you stop them?" she shouted.

"It's three against three," said Tom. "Let them fight it out."

Lucy made her way among the fighting boys to Sam's side. She grabbed his clenched fist. "Stop that this instant," she said.

The boy on the bottom suddenly arched his body and dislodged Sam, who fell heavily to the ground. Then he scrambled to his feet and ran down the street, followed by two of the others. When he reached the corner, he stopped and called back, "Dirty old Republicans!"

Sam got to his feet and glared at Lucy, his hands on his hips. "Why'd you go and spoil the fight?" he asked. "We were winning. Any second he'd have hollered 'uncle!' "

One of the boys picked up the pieces of chalk that lay on the ground. He handed one to Sam, then walked over to the rough board fence and printed 'Roosevelt and Fairbanks' in big, uneven letters.

The other boy stood over some words that had been chalked on the walk and began to rub them off with the sole of his shoe. He looked up at Sam. His face was dirty and a trickle of blood crept from one nostril. "I guess we showed them!" he said.

"Let's get back to work," said Sam. "So long, Lucy." He took a step down the street.

"Just a minute, Sam Snow," Lucy called. "You're not going anywhere before you tell me what this is all about."

Sam turned around and came back. "Aw, these kids have been stealing chalk from school all week. Me and George heard them talking about it. They said they would write 'Parker and Davis' all over town." He shook his head. "We couldn't let them do that." Sam fingered his eye, which had turned black and was beginning to swell. "So we got some chalk of our own and followed them all morning. Every time they wrote 'Parker and Davis,' we rubbed it out and wrote 'Roosevelt and Fairbanks.' "

George finished with the wall and joined the group. "We had just begun work here," he said, "when they came around the corner and started throwing rocks." He rubbed his back. "One of them hit me right here."

"The Loyal Republican Army," said Tom. "Looks as if you've won." He laughed.

"Wait until Mother sees your knickers, Sam," said Lucy. "You won't feel so victorious then."

Sam examined his leg. A three-inch triangle of cloth hung down, exposing the gray woolen underwear beneath. He scowled. "Guess I'll give these pants to the cause," he said. His face brightened. "Maybe I'll get a beefsteak for my eye." He looked at his friends. "Come on, let's go," he said, "we're wasting time." He waved at Lucy. "I'll be home when the chalk's gone," he called, and the three boys ran down the streets.

"Sam's a real scrapper," said Tom as he watched the disheveled back disappear around the corner.

"I don't know why he has to fight all the time," said Lucy. "I think it's disgusting."

They walked back toward the bonfire. Tom edged around her so that he was on the outside, next to the street. Just like a gentleman with his lady, thought Lucy, and the idea made her a little nervous.

"What did you expect Sam to do when they started throwing rocks?" asked Tom.

"But he kept on hitting that boy after he was flat on the ground," said Lucy. "I don't think it was fair."

"He would have stopped anytime the other boy yelled 'uncle,'" said Tom, "and the other boy knew it."

They reached the bonfire, and Tom took Lucy's elbow as they stepped off the curb. He let go as soon as both her feet were solidly on the street, but for the first time Lucy was aware that he treated her like a girl.

"I don't like fighting," she said, suddenly afraid to let a silence grow. "It's ugly."

"If you're going to be a politician, you'll have your share of fights," he said. "Remember the trouble in the park."

Lucy frowned. This wasn't the kind of politics they had talked about in civics class. "But Aunt Letitia didn't fight," she said. "She left the platform."

"You won't always be able to do that," said Tom. "Besides, you're too nice to get messed up with those old ladies." He kept his eyes fixed on the bonfire.

"Don't worry, Tom," said Lucy, her cheeks as pink as her hair ribbon. "It'll be thirty years before I look like Aunt Letitia."

Tom smiled. "I wouldn't be too sure," he said. "She was awfully pretty on the posters."

Their laughter echoed across the yard and Lucy was suddenly at ease. But she had so many things to think about. And politics was only one of them.

XVI

A STRANGE BUGGY stood in front of the house. Thin
red stripes decorated its gleaming black sides and rubber
tires protected the iron wheels. Tucked in the harness,
just over the ear of the splendid black horse, was a gold
chrysanthemum.

Lucy walked closer and looked inside. The leather
upholstery smelled rich and new, and the green velvet
carpet was spotless — except for a piece of paper that
lay in one corner. She picked it up and turned it over.
The familiar words leaped out: Help women get the
vote. Aunt Letitia had left her trail. She had been in
this buggy.

The sound of voices made her jump. A man was
backing out of the front door, and she heard Aunt
Letitia bid him a cordial goodbye. Jonathan Harrison

walked down the steps and as he passed her, he tipped his hat.

Lucy was mystified. When he had come for dinner, he had exchanged only a few words with her aunt. And Aunt Letitia had been openly scornful of bachelors paraded for her benefit.

She hurried into the house and ran into the parlor, where Aunt Letitia had picked up her knitting and was counting stitches.

"What was Mr. Harrison doing here?" she asked.

Her aunt smiled. "He bought a new buggy and wanted to show it off," she said. "Jonathan is a very pleasant man."

Lucy waited, but only the click of needles broke the silence. "I spent the morning working for women," she said.

"What do you mean?" asked Aunt Letitia.

"Sam took a pile of leaflets from your room the other night," said Lucy. "I gave them out at the grocery store."

Her aunt laid down her knitting. "And . . ." she said.

"And women took them," said Lucy. "I gave away every one."

"Were they pleased?" asked her aunt.

"Some were, and some became angry," said Lucy. "Mrs. Smith said I was passing out garbage and told Mr. Johnson to run me away from the store. And I gave one to Mr. Amberson." She flushed at the memory. "He told me to forget that twaddle and go back to my games."

"That made you angry, didn't it?" said Aunt Letitia.

"Yes, but I don't care what they say. I intend to keep on working for woman suffrage. Why are all men so dead set against it?"

"Not all men are," said her aunt. "Jonathan drove me around to distribute leaflets this morning." She blushed and bent her head over her knitting.

"Tom promised to help me, too," said Lucy, "but he said that he didn't want his mother — or his wife — to be a suffragist." She fell silent and traced a feathery scroll in the red carpet with her toe.

Aunt Letitia purled a row. Then she said, "Tom is important to you, isn't he?"

"He's just a good friend," said Lucy. "He comes over here to see Sam as much as me."

"If that's so," said her aunt, "why does he spend so much time on your campaign for class secretary? He should be working on his own. And why did he promise to help you give out those leaflets? Tom thinks a lot of you."

Lucy turned this idea over in her mind. The more she thought about it, the more she liked it. It explained some of the remarks Tom had made.

Aunt Letitia watched her closely but did not say a word.

At last Lucy said, "Tom is important to me."

"More important than the vote?" asked her aunt.

"No. . . ." said Lucy hesitantly. "I don't think so." She frowned. Her aunt was giving her Tom with one hand and taking him back with the other.

"It's one of the drawbacks to working for suffrage," said Aunt Letitia. The needles clicked as slowly as she spoke. "Few men are willing to have their wives make speeches or ring doorbells. They want them home in the kitchen and the nursery." She gazed into the distance. "That's why I never married."

"I expect I'll never get married either," said Lucy. But the words that would have been decisive yesterday sounded hesitant this afternoon. "I'll be the first woman governor of New York," she said in a firmer voice.

"The best way to begin," said her aunt, "is to win that class election. It's good practice."

"I'll have to do better on Monday than I did at the speech assembly," said Lucy.

"That taught you to prepare your talks ahead of time," said Letitia. "You'll never face another crowd without a speech."

Lucy nodded. "Never," she said.

"Does Will know what you've been up to this morning?" asked her aunt.

This was a topic Lucy preferred not to think about. "No," she said slowly. "He didn't ask me what I was doing and I didn't tell him."

"He's sure to find out. And he's forbidden anything of the sort."

Lucy shifted uneasily on the sofa cushion. "But I must help," she said, "and . . ."

The parlor door flew open and Father walked into the room. She froze and waited for him to shout at her. Perhaps Mr. Amberson or Mrs. Smith had stopped him to complain of her leaflets.

But Father was in a good humor. "I'm glad to see you're getting some sense, Letitia," he said. "I understand you've been out riding with Jonathan Harrison."

"That's right," said Aunt Letitia. A smile hovered at the corner of her lips.

"Now maybe you'll forget this suffragette nonsense and settle down," he said.

Aunt Letitia looked at her brother over her spectacles. "One buggy ride doesn't make a marriage," she said calmly.

Father tugged at his mustache. Lucy knew he was remembering the buggy ride with Judge Clark twenty-five years ago.

"Of course not," he said, "but Jonathan Harrison is a catch for any woman."

Aunt Letitia stood up. "At least his head isn't full of fool ideas," she said. "Lucy, I think Maud needs our help in the kitchen."

She marched out of the parlor with Lucy close at her heels.

XVII

P<small>RAISE</small> F<small>ATHER</small>, Son and Holy Ghost. Amen." The
last notes of the Doxology died away and the Reverend
Hinckley stepped into the pulpit. Coughs and the rustle
of skirts rippled through the white frame church as the
congregation settled itself for the sermon.

Lucy scooted closer to Mother, for the air was cold
and the potbellied stove in the back of the church did
not warm the parishioners in the front rows. The words
of the sermon became a steady drone and Lucy no longer
listened. She leaned forward and took a hymnal from
the rack. While the minister preached on, she leafed
idly through the book, stopping to read the familiar
hymns, though she knew them by heart.

On the other side of Father, Sam wriggled in his seat.

He began to tap the next pew rhythmically with the toe of his shoe. At the same moment that the woman who sat in front of him turned and frowned, Father put his hand on Sam's knee. The rapping stopped and Sam slumped, arms folded across his chest and legs stretched out, far under the other pew.

The words from the pulpit broke into Lucy's rendition of "A Mighty Fortress Is Our God," which she was mentally singing in a deep baritone. She closed the book with a snap and began to listen.

"Time and time again," said the minister, "I hear it said that woman suffrage is evil because the Bible forbids it. But nowhere does the Bible say, 'Woman, thou shalt not vote.' "

Lucy raised her head and looked at her aunt. They both broke into smiles and Aunt Letitia winked. Out of the corner of her eye, Lucy could see that Father was staring straight ahead.

"True," the minister went on, "Paul says that the wife is subject to the husband, but that is no reason to deny her the vote. Paul also says that every person is subject to the governing authorities. If we deny woman the ballot because she is subject to her husband, we must also deny man the ballot because he is subject to the government."

At last the Reverend Hinckley had the full attention of the congregation. Not a soul fidgeted, even Sam listened.

"Why is it," asked the minister, "that we are frequently reminded of Paul's words that make the husband the head of the household, yet none of you ever repeats the other side of Paul's advice?" He pointed at a pew where several of the deacons sat together. "Paul also said, 'woman is not independent of man nor man of woman; for as woman was made from man, so man is now born of woman.' And in Ephesians he declared, 'husbands should love their wives as their own bodies.'

"And how do some of us, many of us, show that love?" he asked. He pounded on the pulpit. "We keep our wives in virtual slavery and behave like savages when they protest against the chains."

Father cleared his throat and ran his finger along the inside of his collar. A loud sniff came from the front row, where Mr. and Mrs. Smith sat with Mabel and Walter.

"On Thursday night this entire town was disgraced," said the minister, "when a group of men and boys behaved like runaways from a reform school. As you know, they insulted a woman, a lone woman who was only trying to exercise her right to speak."

By now Father was twisting the end of his mustache between his fingers, his eyes never leaving the minister's face. Every spine in the church stood upright, as if Mr. Richardson had straightened each one with his carpenter's plumb line.

"You may oppose woman suffrage," the voice from the

pulpit now thundered. "You have every right to do that. But, my friends, never dare to cloak your opposition in the words of God!" The Reverend Hinckley raised his hands; the thunder died away, and his voice became as gentle as soft spring rain. "Let us pray," he said.

The prayer was short and the notes of the last hymn tinkled from the old upright piano in the corner. Only the minister's baritone and the cracked soprano of the pianist sang the first few bars. Then the congregation, recovering from their shock, joined in.

"The Old Rugged Cross" was one of Lucy's favorite hymns, but she sang automatically, paying no attention to the words. She could hardly wait to get outdoors and hear what Father and the others had to say about the sermon.

Before the last notes trailed away, people streamed out of the church door and down the steps. They paused briefly to shake the minister's waiting hand, but few had more than a brief good morning for him. They saved their words for the buzzing groups that swarmed over the churchyard. The ladies who sat at the makeshift table selling tickets for the annual turkey dinner might have been lost in the Sahara desert. No one was half so interested in next week's dinner as they were in the morning's sermon.

Beside the church steps, the grocer and Dr. Appleton had their heads together. In a voice that carried across the churchyard, Dr. Appleton said, "You can bet your life that six months after the women get the vote you won't be able to buy a drink of whiskey anywhere in the country."

Mr. and Mrs. Smith stood on the grass, talking with two of the deacons. As Lucy walked by, she heard Mrs. Smith say, "At least he was clever enough to pass the collection plate *before* he preached."

Near the bed of bronze chrysanthemums Aunt Letitia and Jonathan Harrison were talking quietly. The hat she had borrowed from Mother was becoming, and her gold spectacles were tucked into her purse. A dimple showed in her cheek.

While Mother and Mrs. Rasmussen decided how many pumpkin pies they would need for the turkey dinner, Lucy shifted uneasily from one foot to the other.

Under the maple trees stood Mr. Amberson and Father, Mr. Amberson shaking a finger at Father, who tugged hard at his mustache. She was sure that they were talking about the leaflets. And just as sure that Father would want to have a word with her when they reached home.

"What are you fidgeting about?" said a voice behind her.

"Hello, Tom," she said. "I wondered where you were." Her hand stole up to straighten her hair.

"I don't know if you have God on your side," said Tom with a grin, "but you sure have the minister."

They walked across the frost-tarnished lawn to the

edge of the street. Sinner nickered softly and Lucy stepped over to the buggy and stroked his velvet nose.

"This morning Mother asked why we always ride behind Sinner on Sunday," Lucy said, "and Father answered that a Sinner needed church a lot more than a Saint."

Before she could tell Tom about Mr. Amberson, Mother and the Bryans joined them. "We're going to the Bryans' for dinner," said Mother, "so Tom can ride with us."

Tom helped Mother and Lucy into the buggy and climbed in beside them. It rocked as Father swung himself into the driver's seat. He gave Lucy a long look before he picked up the reins.

Mr. Harrison gallantly lent Aunt Letitia a hand into his buggy. But before he climbed up beside her, he paused to wipe a smudge off the gleaming black handrail.

"Ready whenever you are," he called out.

"Where's Sam?" asked Mother. "I declare, that boy is never around when you want him."

"I expect he's showing off his black eye," said Father with a chuckle.

Just then Sam ran across the churchyard and clambered aboard. As Sinner picked up his hoofs and started down the street, Lucy settled nervously into the cushion. Father knew exactly what she had done yesterday.

XVIII

THE AFTERNOON SUN slanted between the velvet dra-
peries into the Bryans' parlor. As Mr. Bryan lifted his
cigar to his mouth, the rays shone on his gold signet
ring. He and Father sat opposite each other in soft
upholstered chairs, pleasantly uncomfortable from too
many helpings of pot roast and apple pie. Mother and
Mrs. Bryan talked together on the plush sofa, protected
from the prickly fabric by their long full skirts. Aunt
Letitia and Mr. Harrison were out in the new buggy
again.

Lucy and Tom and Sam sat in a half-circle in front
of the fireplace, their heads bent over the Ouija board,
their fingers resting on the small wooden planchette
that moved across the surface to spell out mysterious
messages.

118

"Your turn, Sam," said Tom.

"Just a minute," said Sam. He rubbed his freckled nose and thought. "I got it," he said. "Will Lucy be elected secretary tomorrow?"

Three pairs of eyes followed every twitch of the wooden triangle as it began to move over the polished surface. Beneath their fingers, it glided across the alphabet to the top of the board and hesitated. It skittered to the left and stopped over the word, "yes."

"Congratulations, Miss Secretary," said Tom. "I told you that you could beat Mabel Smith."

Lucy shook her head. "Let's try it again," she said. She closed her eyes and concentrated. "Will I be secretary of the ninth grade?" she asked. For a long time the planchette remained motionless, then it moved again to the top of the board. This time it stopped over the word "no."

"Aw, you pushed it," said Sam. "That's not fair."

"I did not!" said Lucy. "It moved by itself." She took her fingers from the planchette and settled her dress. "It just proves the old thing doesn't work. I'm tired of this game, anyway. Can't we play something else?"

It made her uneasy to have a piece of dumb wood predict her future. She half believed in the power of the board and to catch it in error, saying yes and no at the same time, relieved her misgivings.

"I'll get the Parcheesi," said Tom. He carried the Ouija box over to the mahogany sideboard. While he searched for the Parcheesi set, Lucy began to listen to the men.

"At first I thought my sister was Smithville's only problem," said Father, stroking his mustache. "But after today's sermon, I am beginning to wonder."

Mr. Bryan puffed on his cigar. "The preacher had better let politics alone," he said, "and stick to things he knows something about."

"Yes," said Father, nodding his head. "He's supposed to save our souls, not tell us how to vote."

Tom laid the Parcheesi board on the hearth, but Lucy shook her head and put her fingers to her lips. Mother and Mrs. Bryan had stopped talking and were listening to their husbands. A frown creased Mother's forehead.

"You can tell that he has no business of his own to manage," said Mr. Bryan, who ran the feed and grain store. "Put him in charge of a business, and he'd go broke in three months." He blew a series of fat smoke rings that rose lazily in the air.

"I guess the whole town will turn out to hear Senator Throckmorton speak on Wednesday," said Father.

Lucy began to distribute the colored markers to Tom and Sam. But she had to bite her lip to keep from speaking out.

She paid little attention to the game and missed all her chances to defeat Sam or Tom. Over and over she heard Father's and Mr. Bryan's words about the minister, and each time she remembered them she became angrier. Never had she felt so cross with Father. His mind was closed and he would not listen to anyone who disagreed with him. He was as prejudiced about females as he was about Democrats. Democrats might as well be criminals and women nothing but galley slaves.

Mr. Bryan's voice changed the subject. "How did Sam get that shiner?" he asked.

Father chuckled and looked proudly at his son. "A chip off the old block, John," he said. "He was doing a little campaigning for Roosevelt and met up with some Democrat ruffians. They started a fight and he finished it."

"Good for him," said Mr. Bryan. "Tell you what. I'm on the committee for the Senator's visit. You bring that boy around just before the parade, and I'll see that he meets the Senator."

Lucy glared at her brother, who was intent on the Parcheesi board and had heard none of the conversation. He shook the cup, threw the dice, and they rattled to a stop.

"I win!" he shouted. "It's a three." He moved his last counter home and gave Lucy a gloating smile.

She wanted to hit him. "You would, baby," she said angrily.

"What's the matter?" asked Tom. "He won fair and square."

"I don't want to talk about what baby does," said Lucy. She picked up the dice and the counters and put them into the box.

Sam looked bewildered. "All I did was win the game," he said.

Just then Father stood up. "It's time we were getting home," he said.

They bundled on their coats and moved toward the door. For the fifth time Mother told Mrs. Bryan how good the dinner was. As they started across the porch, Tom grabbed Lucy's hand.

"Calm down, Lucy," he whispered. "Don't take it out on Sam." He squeezed her fingers. "So long, see you at the next election."

Lucy smiled in spite of herself. "Goodbye, Mr. Treasurer," she called, and followed Mother to the carriage.

XIX

ALL THE WAY HOME Lucy sat stiffly in the corner of the buggy. She was outraged at what she had overheard in the Bryans' parlor, but a new feeling crept deeper into her anger. She became uneasy over what Mr. Amberson had said in the churchyard — and, worse, what Father was going to do about it.

Father gave no hint that he knew about Lucy's adventure. His mind appeared to be on his digestion.

"That woman will never learn to make a decent pie crust," he said and gently prodded his stomach. "Feels like a lump of lead in my middle."

"I'll give you some baking soda as soon as we get home," said Mother. She leaned forward and patted him on the arm.

Father smiled at Mother over his shoulder and shook the reins, urging Sinner briskly up the driveway. While he unharnessed the horse and settled him in his stall, the rest of the family trooped through the back door. The house was nearly as cold as the outdoors. There had been no heat in the parlor all day and the kitchen, where traces of the breakfast fire lingered, was the only room that did not feel like an Alaskan igloo.

Before Mother fixed Father's soda, she started a fire in the range. Lucy picked up her Latin grammar and sat down uncomfortably at the kitchen table.

The sound of Father scraping his shoes on the back stoop tied a knot in her stomach. She stared at the page of irregular verbs and did not look up when he opened the back door.

"That feels good," he said. "It's cold in the stable."

He took off his gloves and blew on his hands. Then he picked up the glass of soda and water and drank it in one gulp. Lucy lowered her head close to the page.

Father struck his checkered vest with his fist and politely belched. "Thanks, Maud," he said. "I feel better already."

He walked over to the table and stood beside Lucy, who was mumbling Latin verbs beneath her breath. He stood there for a long time.

At last he said, "I thought I told you to confine your politics to school."

She raised her head from her book as if she had been

totally absorbed in her Latin. "What did you say?" she asked.

"You heard me," Father answered. "Did you disobey me yesterday?" His voice was stern and the hard lines around his eyes and mouth frightened Lucy.

She gripped the book. "Yes, Father," she said hesitantly, "I did disobey you." She looked down at the print on the page, which swam into a meaningless jumble.

"I'll not have a daughter of mine making a fool of herself in this way." He leaned over her. "Listen to me, Lucy," he said, emphasizing each word. "This is not one of your escapades that can be laughed off. You're meddling with serious things this time."

"I had to do it, Father," said Lucy in a small voice.

"What do you mean, you had to do it?"

She looked up at him and tears began to gather. "It's unfair to treat women so," she said. "They should have the vote."

"Unfair, is it?" said Father. "Your Aunt Letitia has been corrupting your mind. I can see I'm going to have to have a talk with that woman."

Tears were now rolling down Lucy's cheeks. "It's not Aunt Letitia," she said. "It's the way you and all the other men in the country act. You're unfair." She dashed the tears away and with a toss of her head threw her braids over her shoulder. "Sam gets into politics and you say he's a chip off the old block. I get into politics and you say that I'm a thankless child who's made a fool of herself." She gazed steadily at Father and refused to drop her eyes.

He was speechless. Several times he opened his mouth, but not a word came out.

Lucy stood up. "You can do anything you like," she said. The tears stopped. "But I intend to help the suffragists every chance I get."

Father pointed toward the stairs with a shaking finger. "Go to your room, young lady," he shouted. "And stay there until you're ready to be respectful to your elders."

Lucy walked by his outstretched arm and out of the kitchen. She wanted to run upstairs as fast as her legs would carry her, but she knew that this was no time to act like a child. She felt Father's eyes on her and head thrown back, chin up and eyes straight ahead, she climbed the stairs with a stiff dignity.

When the door closed behind her with a satisfying bang, ringing down the curtain on her performance, she sagged. Then she ran over to her bed and buried her face in the pillow. What would Father do? Never before had she spoken to him like that, but she would not take back a word of it.

Perhaps she would spend the rest of her life a prisoner in this room. She looked around at all the familiar objects — her old doll that sat in the corner, her books, the picture of Alice Longworth Roosevelt that she had torn out of the *Ladies' Home Journal* and pinned to her wall.

She imagined the sound of a key in the lock, the sliding of a bolt and Mother, a ring of keys at her waist, bringing a tray of bread and water for the prisoner. And Lucy, her hair grown as long as Rapunzel's, seated at the window, looking out at a world she could never hope to enter. Her tears began to fall once more at the thought of the lovely young prisoner confined to a lonely room by her wicked father.

After a time she raised her head from her pillow and propped her chin on her hand. The tears dried as she began to imagine clever things she might have said to Father, such intelligent statements of women's rights that he would have begged her pardon for ever saying that suffragists were foolish or unnatural.

She walked over to her bureau and looked into the mirror. An ugly girl with red, puffy eyes stared back at her. Lucy poured water from the china pitcher into the basin that stood on the walnut washstand, shuddering as she splashed the icy water on her face.

The sound of loud voices from below made her put down the washcloth and tiptoe to her door. She opened it a crack and heard Father's words.

"I don't care if you are my own sister," he shouted, "as long as you're under my roof, you'll not meddle with my daughter's mind."

Aunt Letitia's voice was calm. "That's the trouble with you, Will," she said. "You act as if you owned Lucy. She's a person with a mind of her own. If you weren't such a pig-headed fool, she wouldn't be so determined. You're a living, breathing argument for women's rights."

"Lucy was never mixed up in this kind of crazy scheme before you came to town," Father said.

"She's nearly grown," said Aunt Letitia. "You can't keep her a baby forever. She needs no one to give her ideas. When she got Maud to take her to the park, she hadn't an inkling that I was the speaker."

"She can't make speeches from upstairs," said Father. "If it's the only way to keep her out of politics, I'll see that she stays in her room all winter."

Heavy footsteps sounded on the kitchen floor. As they came nearer, Lucy shut the door.

If she had to stay in her room until she promised never to work for woman suffrage, she would stay in her room forever. But she wished she had her school books upstairs so that she could finish her homework for tomorrow.

XX

THE SUN was still below the mountains when Lucy looked out her window. But the air was rosy and a sparrow chirped on a bare tree limb. No matter how she tried to cling to yesterday's defiance, it slipped away in the freshness of the morning.

As she pulled her petticoat over her head, she resolved to be polite and respectful, no matter how she disagreed with Father. But by the time she had wound a shoelace around the hooks on one high-topped shoe and tied it with a jerk that broke the string, she was as firmly resolved not to back down from her vow to help women win the vote.

No one was around when she opened her door, but her foot stopped in midair above the first step at the sound of Mother's voice.

"You were too hard on Lucy," said Mother.

Lucy could tell by the sounds that came from the bedroom that Mother was combing her hair. Her voice was muffled as if she spoke through a mouthful of hairpins.

"If you forbid Lucy to get into politics, it's hardly fair to reward Sam for the same thing," she said.

Lucy waited for Father's reply. After a long time he said, "How does it look when I can't control my own daughter? I'll be the laughing stock of Smithville."

There was another long silence and then in a clear voice Mother said, "Do you *really* think so, Will?"

The clatter of the comb on the bureau sent Lucy scurrying down the stairs and into the kitchen. Father had started the fire an hour before and the room was cozy. She measured the small brown beans from the painted wooden canister into the coffee mill. When she turned the crank, the fragrance filled the room like perfume.

Father's deep voice said, "Nothing like the smell of fresh-ground coffee."

"Good morning, Father," said Lucy. She held tightly to the handle of the mill and waited.

Father said nothing except "What a beautiful morning." He said nothing at all while Mother cut lard into flour for biscuits, nothing while she fried eggs in spluttering grease, and nothing while the heaped platters were carried to the table. At breakfast he talked only about the good food, but Lucy noticed that he ate no more than three biscuits and refused a second plateful of sausage and eggs.

Not until he went out to the stable to hitch Saint and Sinner to the dray did Lucy relax. When she carried the stacked dishes into the kitchen, she found herself singing. And her gay spirits lasted all the way to school in spite of the tiny voice deep inside that whispered that nothing had been settled.

The school yard buzzed with excitement. Everyone seemed to have forgotten Aunt Letitia's wild night in the park. They talked only about the day's election, when they would choose their class officers.

Lucy joined Tom and a group that called encouragement to a boy who scrubbed at the sidewalk. A big red, white and blue banner blossomed on the side of the building. George Parker, who hoped to be the next twelfth grade president, had found a "Judge Parker for President" poster, and sometime over the weekend he had hung it in the school yard. The word "Judge" had been covered with a crudely painted "George," and it was plain to see that the painting had been done after the banner was fastened to the wall.

Splashes of red paint trailed across the banner, the building and the sidewalk below. George was on his hands and knees, cleaning the scarlet smudges with a rag and a bottle of turpentine. Over him stood Mr. Amberson, twisting his shaggy eyebrow between his thumb and forefinger as he watched to make sure that George removed every speck of paint.

The memory of Lucy's last meeting with the principal brought a flush to her cheek. "Just like that mean old Mr. Amberson," she said, "to spoil somebody's fun."

Tom turned his head sharply and stared at Lucy. "Why shouldn't George have to clean up his own mess?" he asked.

"No reason, I guess," said Lucy slowly. It was hard to admit that Mr. Amberson might be right. "No reason at all." She tossed the end of her muffler over her shoulder and shifted her school books to her other arm. "And there's no reason for me to stand and watch," she said, walking away.

"What's wrong, Lucy?" asked Tom. "Are you upset about the election?"

"That's the least of my worries." She told Tom about her argument with Father. "But this morning he acted as if nothing had happened," she said.

"Maybe it's all right," said Tom. "Maybe if you don't aggravate him, he'll forget all about it."

"Don't you see that the only way I can get along with Father is to pretend? When I'm honest I get sent to my room. Or worse."

There was no answer. They crossed the yard in silence and walked up the steps. Several girls who came from the opposite direction met them in front of the door.

One of them looked at Lucy and laughed. "Be careful," said Mabel Smith, "it's that dreadful suffragette. Don't get too near, she might infect you." She swept into the building, followed by the giggling girls.

"Mabel's mother must have talked about meeting you," said Tom. "Mabel will see that every person at Smithville High hears about it by noon."

"Her mother probably said that I ripped her skirt. But I'm willing to take the credit." Tom held the door open for her. "Let's find a quiet place. I want to finish my Latin before the bell."

All through her morning classes Lucy thought about Mabel and the school election. And about her meeting with Mrs. Smith. It would soon be time to vote and she knew that she wanted to win. It seemed very important.

When she stepped back onto the school grounds after dinner, Joe McBroom got up, stumbled over a stack of school books and walked over to meet her.

"I hear you've been giving Mrs. Smith fits," he said. "Keep it up, Lucy."

"Sure, Joe," she mumbled. The school bell rang, rescuing her, as she stood there with nothing sensible to say.

All through civics she wondered why Joe had been so friendly. He had said such nasty things about Aunt Letitia that she would have expected him to call her a crowing hen for meddling in men's affairs. She concentrated so hard upon Joe's words that when Miss Harrington asked her to recite the powers of Congress, she could not remember a single one.

At last it was time for algebra. Mr. Chester came into the room and began to write the assignment on the blackboard. Lucy fidgeted in her seat and tapped her pencil nervously on the side of her desk. Surely he knew that the class elections were scheduled for this period.

Mr. Chester copied the last page number onto the board, ended with a flourish of chalk, and turned to face the class. He looked at Lucy, holding his gaze steady until she blushed and put her pencil down.

"It appears that the candidates are somewhat nervous," he said. "I suppose we should vote and get it over with."

He took a stack of ballots from his briefcase and began to pass them out. "For those of you who are concerned with this election," he said, "the votes should all be counted by four-thirty. The results will be posted on Mr. Amberson's door."

Lucy dipped a pen into her inkwell and made a bold X on her ballot opposite Bill Bishop for class president. Her eye moved down the list and she pondered over the vice president, hesitating between two names, then marked an x after Margaret Peters.

Now her own name was in front of her, just below the words, Mabel Smith. She postponed her vote for a moment and glanced around the classroom. At this second her name was before every eye in each ninth grade class. She dipped her pen again and her hand hovered over the ballot. How odd it was to be choosing yourself. She wondered if Theodore Roosevelt felt funny when he voted for himself.

She made the X after her name, then cast her vote for Tom as treasurer. Carefully she blotted the paper, folded it neatly in half and put her pen away.

Lucy's gaze followed each ballot as it traveled from desk to desk and at last reached Mr. Chester. She could hardly tear her eyes away as he stuffed the ballots into his leather brief case. How could she wait until four-thirty?

XXI

THE VARNISHED WALNUT DOOR was closed. At eye
level was a shiny brass plate inscribed LLEWELLYN P.
AMBERSON, PRINCIPAL.

Lucy had been staring at the door for nearly an hour.
Leaning against the wall nearby, she and Tom waited
for the results of the class election. The other candidates
were standing around in the corridor, but Lucy made no
effort to talk to them.

"Surely Mr. Amberson has finished counting," she
said. "I'm getting awfully tired."

"So am I," Tom said. He moved his books along the
corridor and sat down on the floor with his back to the
wall. "Why don't you make yourself comfortable?"

Lucy hesitated. She could hear Mother's voice

plainly: "Ladies don't sit on the floor." She glanced up and down the hall, looking for teachers. With a shrug of her shoulders, she slid down and stretched her long legs out into the corridor.

She wiggled her toes inside her shoes. "That does feel better," she said.

"How's the suffragist business going?" Tom asked.

"Terrible," said Lucy. She rubbed her forehead and sighed. "I told you about Father this morning, and all you could say was not to aggravate him. Nobody understands."

Tom started to speak, but Lucy gave him no chance to say a word.

"Aunt Letitia stood up for me," she said, "but she's so busy buggy-riding with Jonathan Harrison that she's forgotten everything else."

Before Tom could answer, the door across the hall opened and Mr. Amberson strode out, Mr. Chester and two other teachers close at his heels. With a flourish he fixed the white sheet exactly in the center of the door, below the nameplate.

Tom scrambled to his feet and held out his hand. As he pulled Lucy up, he smiled as if he'd rather hold her hand than be class treasurer. The new Tom that she kept seeing since her talk with Aunt Letitia was more exciting than her old friend.

From up and down the hall students surged toward the principal's door. Lucy closed her eyes. Once she

137

had read the names on that paper, the election would be officially over, but until she saw the words Mabel Smith, Secretary, she could still hope.

Slowly she opened her eyes and began to read the list, forcing herself to start at the top. Each word was written with the scrolls and flourishes of Mr. Amberson's finest penmanship. Her glance swept over the first three groups. Sidewalk-scrubbing George Parker had been elected president of the twelfth grade. Now she had reached the ninth grade officers. Her mouth grew dry as she began to read the names: President, James Casey.

Before she could move on to the next list, Tom shouted, "We've won, Lucy! Look, we've won!"

Lucy looked. There in bold print, plain as day, were the words: Secretary, Lucy Snow; Treasurer, Tom Bryan. All around her was tumult, but Lucy could only stand and silently stare at the two names that danced before her eyes.

Tom took her by the arm and steered her out of the crowd. They picked up their books and went down the corridor, Lucy walking on pink, fleecy clouds that floated a foot above the floor.

"You should be jumping up and down and hollering," said Tom. "Why so quiet?"

"I was so sure I would lose," said Lucy. "I messed up my speech and made a fool of myself. I still don't believe I have won. I just can't understand."

"Mabel elected you. She couldn't have helped you more if you had paid her," said Tom.

"What do you mean? Mabel never did anything for me."

"Not out of the goodness of her heart," said Tom, "but out of spite." He held the door open and they walked down the steps. "Mabel spent the entire morning spreading the word about the horrible suffragette Lucy Smith who made her dear mother so angry."

Lucy frowned. "But how did that help?"

"A lot of the fellows thought that if you could stand up to that old shrew," said Tom, "you had the kind of spunk they wanted in a class officer. Mabel must have won at least twenty votes for you."

Lucy was thoughtful, matching her stride to Tom's. Would Father be so pleased with her victory that he would forget her politics? She hoped so, but right now it didn't matter. More important was the fact that she had won — and the pressure of Tom's hand on her elbow as they crossed the street.

XXII

Aᴲᴛᴇʀ sᴜᴘᴘᴇʀ the family gathered in the parlor. Jonathan Harrison sat beside Aunt Letitia, who made no move to take her knitting out of the petit point bag beside the sofa. The *New York Times* lay folded on the table while Father and Mr. Harrison talked about the torchlight parade on Saturday.

Sam perched on the footstool beside Father's chair, intent on their words. Since he had learned he would meet Senator Throckmorton, he had been unbearable. He acted as if he were an adult and Lucy a child — or perhaps it was just that he was male and Lucy only female.

Lucy's book rested in her lap, but she read with one ear tuned to the male voices. She looked up as Mother came into the parlor carrying a large tray filled with brimming crystal goblets.

Father stopped in mid-sentence. "What's this?" he asked.

"I thought we should toast the new secretary," said Mother. She offered Lucy one of the glasses of sparkling cider.

"Thank you," said Lucy, bending her head to hide her pleased smile. Little had been said after she first announced her victory, and she had begun to think that no one really cared about the honor.

"Indeed," said Aunt Letitia, taking a glass from the tray. "It's a great occasion when a woman wins an elective office." She waited until everyone had their cider, then she lifted her glass high. "To Lucy," she said, "the next secretary of the ninth grade."

Mr. Harrison stood up, bowed and repeated, "To Lucy."

"To Lucy," said Father, with a tug at his mustache, "a chip off the old block."

Sam scrambled to his feet, bowed so low that his head nearly touched the floor and, sounding like a preacher calling his flock to prayer, intoned, "To Lucy."

Lucy giggled and watched the family drink. Her pleasure was cut short by Sam's next words.

"Too bad she's just a girl," he said. "Old Lucy would be a great politician. She'd give them something to think about."

The gaiety vanished for a moment. Then Aunt Letitia raised her glass once more. "To Lucy," she said, "the
first female senator." She caught Lucy's eye and smiled
as she sipped her cider.

Everyone drank the toast, but the twinkle had left
Father's eye.

Mr. Harrison set his glass on the table and cleared
his throat several times. "I have an announcement to
make," he said. He cleared his throat again.

Father looked at Mother and raised an eyebrow.

"Letitia," said Mr. Harrison, "has honored me by con-
senting to become my wife."

"How wonderful," said Mother. She rushed over to
Aunt Letitia and kissed her on the cheek.

"Congratulations, Jonathan," said Father. He shook
Mr. Harrison's hand. "You're getting a fine woman.
Known her for many years. None finer."

"Guess I'll have to call you Uncle Jonathan," said
Sam. He pumped Mr. Harrison's hand vigorously.

Not a sound came from Lucy. She sat on her footstool and stared at her aunt. It was past understanding.
After all Aunt Letitia had said about not marrying because she was so devoted to suffrage. Jonathan Harrison
was probably the first man who had ever proposed. And
her aunt had snapped him up like a hungry trout. She
began to worry. If her aunt could have her head turned
by a man with a fancy buggy, what would happen to
Lucy herself? She was bewildered — and afraid.

Suddenly she felt alone in the room. The laughter and talk about her seemed miles away. Father made sounds and laughed and Aunt Letitia looked coy, but it was like the buzzing of a swarm of insects. She looked at the crystal goblet on the table and the glass glittered coldly back at her.

Mother laid her hand on Lucy's shoulder. "You haven't wished your aunt good luck," she said.

Lucy got up and walked slowly across the room. Through stiff, wooden lips she said, "I hope you'll be very happy." She bent and kissed her aunt's cheek.

Aunt Letitia pulled Lucy down beside her. "What's wrong?" she asked.

"Nothing," said Lucy coldly. "Absolutely nothing."

Her aunt patted her on the knee and started to speak when Father's voice boomed across the room.

"I'm glad to see you shook all that suffragist nonsense out of her head, Jonathan," he said.

Lucy looked up at him. He was happier than he had been at any time since the telegram arrived.

"A woman who has a man and a house doesn't run around making speeches and creating a public nuisance," he continued, stroking his mustache.

"Don't be so hasty, Will," said Aunt Letitia. "I'd never marry a man who didn't see eye to eye with me on woman suffrage."

"That's right," said Mr. Harrison. "I've been thinking of organizing some of the businessmen to support the ladies. It's only fair that they should have the vote."

Father's mouth dropped open and his hand fell to his side. "She's bewitched you, too," he said gruffly. "Next thing I hear, you'll be wearing an apron and washing dishes."

Mr. Harrison took Letitia's hand. "If she needed me, I certainly would," he said. "But she'll have someone to do the housework."

Lucy stared at Mr. Harrison. He had ruined everything with his buggy and his flowers and his honeyed phrases. His promises sounded good, but words were cheap. Aunt Letitia seemed as giddy as any empty-headed female wrapped in her chains. How could Aunt Letitia ever marry and still insist on her rights? Lucy raised her goblet to toast the happy couple, but the glass was heavy in her hand and the cider tasted of hemlock.

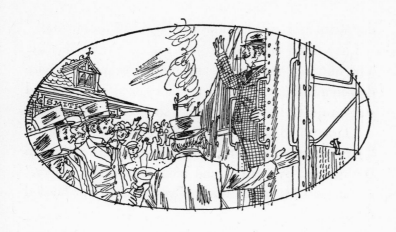

XXIII

FATHER AND SAM nailed a ROOSEVELT AND FAIRBANKS sign across the front porch. "You could see it from the station," said Father proudly, "if that darned elm tree wasn't in the way."

Lucy brought down the flag from the attic. She slipped the pole into the brass standard beside the front door. Mother and Aunt Letitia lowered red, white and blue bunting from the second-story windows for Father to tack to the sills.

When the last nail had been driven into the last banner, they stood in a row and looked up at the house.

"The most patriotic house in the block," pronounced Father. "Letitia, you drape a mighty fine banner."

"Practice, Will," said Aunt Letitia. "When you've

decorated as many platforms as I have, it comes natural."

Lucy tilted her head to one side. It did look nice. The bunting was pleated and fanned below each window in a half-circle. In the center of every sill, Sam had stuck a tin Roosevelt badge that shone like a headlight.

"Time to go," said Father. He looked at his watch. "In twenty-three minutes the Senator's special pulls into the station. We can't stand around here any longer." He slipped his watch into his vest pocket and headed for the stable.

Smithville's great day was about to begin. Far down the track white smoke billowed through the sycamore trees. The rails rumbled, a whistle sounded three short blasts.

"There she is!" shouted a boy from his perch on the ridgepole of the railroad station.

As if tied to a single string of a puppet master, every head on the crowded platform turned to look at the onrushing train. Its whistle blasting, the engine coasted into the station, and the Smithville Municipal Band began a spirited march.

Lucy stood up in the back of the dray, trying to see over the crowd. Father had driven the dray to its usual place at the edge of the platform. Both Saint and Sinner were munching on big feed bags of oats.

With a screech of metal and a sigh of escaping steam, the engine lumbered to a stop. Like a great beast it stood, hissing and spitting water along the track. Red, white and blue bunting festooned the sides of the train, and one enormous banner said ROOSEVELT AND FAIR-BANKS. Another read A SQUARE DEAL FOR EVERY AMER-ICAN.

While the band tooted, heads craned for the first glimpse of Senator Throckmorton. As the last notes died away, a head appeared at the door of the middle car. A moan of relief went up from the crowd, but the head only belonged to the conductor, who opened the gate and put a stool on the ground.

Sam rubbed his eyes from time to time to make sure he would not miss a second of the glorious sight. "Golly," he whispered, "the Senator will step out of that train in just a minute."

Lucy glanced at her brother and sighed with disgust. Just because Sam was to meet the Senator, he acted as if Teddy Roosevelt himself had come to Smithville. After all, it was just a Senator who had come to town, and every state in the union had two of them. Only the bulk of Father, seated stiffly in the dray, twisting the ends of his red mustache, kept her from yielding to a sudden impulse to pull Sam's cap down over his eyes.

A great cheer went up from the crowd as a stout man in a plaid suit and a brown derby appeared in the vesti-bule, climbed down to the waiting stool and raised his arms. Again the people cheered. Four men stepped out of the crowd and hurried forward. Lucy recognized Mayor Whiteside, Judge Clark, Lawyer Gresham and

Mr. Bryan, all looking uncomfortable in their Sunday suits. The Senator shook hands all around and waited, puffing on a big, black cigar, while the Mayor delivered a short speech of welcome.

Father turned and spoke over his shoulder. "It won't be long now, Sam. You'll be meeting the Senator this evening." He beamed proudly. "Mr. Bryan told me to bring you over to Judge Clark's just before the parade."

Sam squirmed with pleasure, his attention fixed on the fat figure in the plaid suit, who until a moment ago had been only a name Father read from the pages of *The New York Times*.

It wasn't fair! The more Lucy watched Sam's and Father's pleasure, the angrier she became. A dark scowl spread over her face. When a ten-year-old boy brawls in the streets and comes home with a black eye, he is treated like a king and introduced to a United States Senator. When a fourteen-year-old girl distributes political pamphlets, she is sent to her room in disgrace. And when she campaigns for a school office — and wins — she is told that "if she were only a man" she could become a State Legislator. It was an unjust world and it was dishonest of men to try to keep it so.

If she weren't a lady, she would hit Sam as hard as she could and wipe that smile off his face.

Suddenly the scene became odious. Her beaming father, the sickening smile on her brother's face, the crowd standing on tiptoe for a glimpse of the performing walrus, the judge and the lawyer bowing and scraping. She wished she had stayed home with Mother, who had said that she felt a headache coming on. She wondered if Aunt Letitia, who sat with Mr. Harrison, felt the same way.

The Mayor finished his speech of welcome and an assistant handed him an enormous key. It was as big as the ruler in Lucy's desk at school, and while it might have unlocked the gates to King Arthur's palace, Lucy was certain there was no keyhole in Smithville that it would fit.

The Senator stuck his cigar into his mouth and accepted the key to the city with one hand and the Mayor's outstretched palm with the other. After a long last puff, he smiled and dropped the cigar.

"That's no nickel smoke," said Father. "Pure Havana at fifty cents, and he tossed it away like a peanut shell."

The Senator thanked the citizens for the key to their fair city, told them what a great President Theodore Roosevelt was, and ended with "Now let's all go over to the park and have some of that barbecue I heard about."

Drums beat and trumpets blared, and the sun glinted on the shiny brass tuba. Following their leader, the band marched forward, scattering the cheering crowd.

Everyone in town — Republicans and Democrats alike — turned out for the barbecue. In a deep pit in the center of the park, a whole ox roasted on a bed of coals until the tender meat was ready to fall from the bones. The butcher and the cook from the Smithville Hotel sliced the beef and piled it high on crusty rolls. Father made the lemonade and, a white apron tied around his ample waist, he presided over great washtubs filled with it.

Mother's headache had vanished. She sat on a bench with Mrs. Rasmussen and Mrs. Hinckley, laughing and talking as if she had never felt a pain.

From time to time Lucy caught a glimpse of Aunt Letitia. Now that she was to be Mrs. Jonathan Harrison, all the ladies in the town were flocking around her. She overheard Aunt Letitia promise the preacher that Mr. Harrison would soon be singing in the choir. But when she saw Mr. and Mrs. Smith talking to the happy pair, she shook her head. What was her aunt thinking about? Didn't she remember Lucy's encounter with that awful woman?

She edged through the crowd, past Sam — who crouched in the dirt, playing mumblety-peg with a group of boys — past Father's lemonade stand, until she could hear her aunt's words.

"So you see," said Aunt Letitia, "what a force for good women could become. The gentle influence of the Christian wife and mother would temper the rash judgments of men."

Mrs. Smith's reply was pleasant. Lucy was amazed. Aunt Letitia would soon have Mrs. Smith writing letters to Washington, demanding the right to vote.

When the Smiths walked away, Aunt Letitia caught sight of Lucy. She waved and Lucy hurried over.

"Are you having a good time?" Aunt Letitia asked.

"Picnics are always fun. But how did you make Mrs. Smith listen to you?"

"You can catch more flies with honey than with vinegar," said her aunt. "Mrs. Smith doesn't care a whit about being oppressed. But she's as weak as water when you talk about what a good Christian woman can do."

Just then Mr. Harrison came back with paper cups of lemonade. The talk turned to the torchlight parade, but Lucy excused herself as soon as she could. It was hard to see Jonathan Harrison as anything but an enemy.

As the afternoon wore on and the kegs of beer were drained, occasional fistfights broke out between Roosevelt and Parker supporters. But for most people, good food prevailed over politics. By dusk the last shred of beef was gone, and the big vat of lemonade was empty.

On the ride home Lucy was tired but happy. Even a slave can be caught up in her master's revels. After all, a United States Senator didn't come to town every day.

XXIV

At the sound of footsteps on the porch, Lucy jumped up from the window seat and ran to the door. That quick step could belong only to Tom. When Father took Sam to meet Senator Throckmorton, he had promised that Tom would stop by for her and Mother.

"This was no night," he had said, "for womenfolk to walk the crowded streets alone."

Lucy opened the door and smiled. "Come in," she said. "We're all ready to go."

Tom took her coat from the hook beside the carved-oak hall rack and held it up. She slipped one hand in, but not the other, fumbling behind her until at last her fingers found the armhole. Tom adjusted the coat and as he smoothed it across her shoulders, their eyes met in the mirror. Lucy blushed and reached for her hat to hide her confusion.

"You look nice," said Tom, never taking his gaze from her as she adjusted the dark blue hat so that the feather stood at a jaunty angle.

Lucy glanced down at her shoes. "Thank you," she said.

"Let's be off for the parade," Mother's voice broke in.

They went gaily down the steps, their breath making frosty trails in the crisp October night. As they walked along, they saw more and more people on the streets. Most of the houses they passed sported flags and pictures of the President. When they turned the corner into Main Street, Lucy caught her breath.

It was like Fairyland. It was like Christmas and Halloween and the Fourth of July all rolled into one. Chinese lanterns decorated the front of every building and hung from ropes looped across the street. Pink and red and yellow and green lanterns glowed like soft balls of fire. Between them hung red, white and blue banners and pictures of President Roosevelt.

The streets were lined with people. From Cooperstown and Johnsonville, from Tarrytown and Bennett's Grove, they had come in buggies and on horseback, by train and on foot, to see the parade and to hear the Senator.

Tom found a place on the curb in front of Harrison's Mercantile. In a few minutes the fire engine's bell clanged through the night and the parade was under way. The horses pulled the big red engine with its load of hose and ladders, and firemen, each dressed in a long rubber overcoat and a shiny red helmet, clung to the truck.

Just as the engine came by, Tom pointed over her head. Lucy looked up and saw a skyrocket burst in the sky above the hotel. Fiery flowers of red and green and blue and gold blotted out the stars. Before the flowers died away, the first marchers strode into view.

Lucy recognized them as men who had come to Smithville with the Senator. Each wore a red, white and blue uniform, tin helmet, shining tin breastplate and oilcloth cape. As they passed, their leader gave a signal. Each marcher blew into a rubber tube. Suddenly gusts of fire flashed and leaped from the tops of every bobbing helmet.

Now skyrockets were bursting so fast that new color spread before the old could fade. Men on horses carried Roman candles that shot balls of colored fire high over the heads of the crowd. New marchers, dressed in bearskin hats and buckskin aprons, held flaming torches. The Smithville Band blared its brassy loudest.

Lucy knew some of the marchers. There was Mr. Johnson, a red, white and blue banner across his chest, an eagle torch that spewed fire from each wing held high above his head. And the druggist, the butcher, the plumber — even the stationmaster was there.

More marchers went past, and then six wagons covered with lanterns and political signs. Out of the backs of the wagons, clusters of Roman candles popped and spurted. From the shouts and laughter, Lucy guessed that the wagoners were celebrating the Senator's arrival with whiskey as well as with fireworks.

A great cheer traveled down the line. Drawn by eight white horses, the Senator's carriage rolled briskly into sight. He stood proudly, resting his great bulk on a silver-headed cane. The face under the tall silk hat smiled back at the crowd and he waved, first to one side of the street, then to the other. As he came to the next corner, girls rushed out and tossed bronze and gold chrysanthemums at his feet. Quickly he plucked the white carnation from his buttonhole and threw it among the girls. Then he pulled off his hat and bowed low in their direction.

His arrival touched off a new wave of fireworks. It seemed as if the whole street was now ablaze with colored fire and the flare of torches.

At last the end of the parade was in sight. It was a band of boys, each holding a torch he had made of cat-tails soaked in kerosene. As they marched by, Lucy suddenly became aware that her hand was in Tom's grasp. She could not remember just when this had happened.

The crowd thinned, but Lucy stood still and stared straight ahead, though it was time to go. She was afraid

155

to turn, afraid that Mother would notice that Tom was holding her hand.

"Goodness, Lucy," said Mother, "are you mesmerized? We have to hurry."

Tom squeezed Lucy's hand and released it. Slowly she turned her head and looked at him. The smile they exchanged was unlike any smile she had ever known. It was as if Tom had gently touched her cheek.

XXV

I THINK we can work our way a little closer," said Tom. He pulled Mother and Lucy along behind him as he threaded his way through the crowd. The throng around the bandstand was packed, but Tom managed to dart between shoulders and hips, opening paths that Lucy couldn't.

"How's this?" he asked.

They stood on a slight rise in the ground, about ten feet from the front. Lucy could see over the heads to the bandstand where empty chairs awaited the Senator and his party.

"That's much better, Tom," said Mother. "It would be too bad if all I saw of the Senator was his tall silk hat."

Only a week ago Lucy had stood here beside Mother and heard the words that had made her both miserable and proud — words that had driven her into a quarrel with Father. Tonight, as she stood between Tom and Mother, she smiled bitterly as she listened to the excited men and women and children. When Aunt Letitia spoke, they came armed with jeers and with rotten eggs. For Senator Throckmorton they turned out the whole town, from the Mayor to the fire brigade. Tonight they honored democracy — last week they had denied it.

Shouts and cheers and music announced the arrival of the Senator. The crowd parted to allow three men with flickering torches to escort the Senator to the stage. Behind him followed his reception committee and the Smithville Municipal Band brought up the rear. As the band passed, the crowd flowed back like the Red Sea after the crossing of the Israelites.

As the Senator mounted the steps Lucy clapped politely, then her hands froze at the sight that met her eyes. There, his foot on the top step, just three paces behind the Senator, was the familiar cap, the carrot curls and the snub nose of her brother. Somehow Sam had become a member of the official party.

"Jeehosophat," said Tom, "isn't that . . ."

"It most certainly is," said Lucy. "The little ruffian's black eye has put him on the platform."

"That's not fair, Lucy," said Mother. She leaned across Tom to speak, and darkness could not hide the

158

concern in her voice. "He worked hard all day for President Roosevelt."

"The Senator's really a great guy," said Tom. "He told Father that he would be delighted to meet Sam." He laughed out loud. "Said the Party needed men who were willing to do battle."

Lucy edged away. For a moment Tom was just another male. She was glad they had not been able to find Father. His pride at Sam's eminence would have been too much to bear.

The last note of the trombones wailed through the park. Judge Clark began to speak, comparing the Senator with Abraham Lincoln and other great benefactors of our fair land. As his words poured out, his voice grew louder. "And we can be sure," he shouted, "that tonight's speech will see none of the disturbance that characterized last week's disgraceful display in this very same park."

"It's plain to see how the Judge feels about you suffragists," said Tom, "but some of us still love you."

It was an effort for Lucy to bite back the words that suddenly rose to her lips. It would be easy to speak sharply and it would make her feel better. But even as her mouth formed the words, she realized that she had no business being angry with Tom.

The Senator's mellow tones rolled across the park. He had earned his reputation as an orator fairly and — against her will — Lucy found herself nodding in agreement. He made it seem as if the United States would reach new heights of glory under a second term with Theodore Roosevelt, that every family would have an automobile, a telephone and electricity, that everlasting peace would spread across the world. And he made it plain that if Parker and Davis were elected, the Republic would perish. Every sentence was interrupted by applause, and once Lucy discovered herself clapping her hands.

But in the blink of an eye, it all changed. The Senator began to speak of the women's crusade. At the word "suffragette," Lucy stiffened. The word was "suffragist" and only people like Father and Mrs. Smith and Mr. Amberson, who thought that votes for women were unnatural or silly, allowed the other term to cross their lips. Surely Senator Throckmorton would rise above prejudice and silly arguments.

The Senator's next words could have been written by Father. "The ladies will always vote just as their husbands do. What woman would support Parker once her husband points out the great benefits of Theodore Roosevelt's leadership? To give the ladies the vote would double the cost of elections. And we must keep taxes down. I tell you, my friends," he said with a chuckle, "it is only economical to restrict the vote to males." Laughter swept across the crowd, and Lucy became indignant.

"That's no reason," she muttered to herself. When

Tom stared at her, she realized that she had spoken out loud.

One by one, the Senator trotted out the stock arguments against suffrage that she had heard repeated by Father and Sam and Joe McBroom and all the males of Smithville. And one by one, Lucy found herself answering them — out loud. After each of the Senator's claims, people around her turned to Lucy, waiting for the replies that rose to her lips. But most of the crowd greeted Senator Throckmorton's statements with applause; as Lucy's resentment deepened, her voice grew louder.

"Consider the fair flower of American womanhood," urged the Senator. "Such delicate blooms have no wish to soil themselves with the vote."

"That's not true!" cried Lucy. "Have you asked us?" With each beautifully shaped syllable that poured from the Senator's mouth, her anger mounted.

"Agitation for the ballot comes," he said, "from a small group of unnatural women who would overturn society and destroy the sanctity of the home. Politics will corrupt the lovely ladies who set the moral tone of our community and woman suffrage will surely lead to a degenerate society."

That was the final straw. A degenerate society indeed. "You're not only a liar," Lucy shouted, "you are an evil man!" She must show the crowd what terrible falsehoods the Senator was spreading.

Against her will, she found her feet moving. Tom grabbed her arm, but she angrily shook off his hand. Mother gasped, "Lucy, what are you doing?" but she paid no attention. She shoved and pushed her way through the crowd, squirming between the closely packed bodies.

"That's not true. That's not true. You've got to listen!" she shouted.

Not a hand was laid upon Lucy as she struggled toward the speaker. Men and women drew back, their eyes wide with astonishment. The entire crowd was motionless, as if a wizard had waved his wand across the park.

She thought of Aunt Letitia — whose words provoked a hail of eggs — and hesitated, but only for a second. Let them do what they liked, she must make them see the truth. On she went, each step taking her closer to the stage.

From the platform, the Senator's words swept across the park, but fewer people heard each sentence. Lucy's struggles were now the center of all eyes.

She reached the stage and climbed the steps. She crossed the wooden floor to the Senator's side. He stared at her as if she were a visitor from Mars. His mouth was open, yet he did not utter a sound. Sam stood up and stretched an arm toward his sister, but he was unable to walk over to her.

Lucy looked out at the crowd, and row after row of

162

pale, upturned faces looked back at her. She shook with righteous indignation, but even as she began to speak, in a tiny corner of her mind a voice repeated in horror, "Lucy Snow, what are you doing?"

"It's a lie," she called out in a small voice, but clearly, "every word the Senator has said about women is a lie."

By now Sam had regained the use of his feet. He rushed across the platform and grabbed her. His eyes were wide as dinner plates as he gasped, "Sit down!"

Without pausing or looking around, she shook him off with a sweep of her arm. Thrown off balance, he staggered back and landed heavily on his bottom. He sat like a statue, watching his sister with horror.

"Women are slaves in this society," continued Lucy. "Those men you have fought to free are permitted to vote, but the mothers of your children are chained to the kitchen. Have you no justice? It is . . ."

The words vanished and she could not finish the sentence. Until now the crowd below her had been a blur, but as her excitement passed, faces came into focus. And the first one she saw was Tom. His face was contorted and he was motioning desperately for her to stop.

Lucy's silence broke the spell. Up the stairs ran the chief of police. Behind him other policemen and several men from the Senator's train shoved their way to the stage. Quickly they surrounded Lucy and hustled her down the steps. They formed a wedge around her with their bodies and pushed straight through the crowd like a locomotive with its throttle open.

Whispers and pointed fingers followed Lucy as she passed, a big policeman on each side of her pulling her along so rapidly that her feet hardly touched the ground.

"That's Will Snow's daughter." The words struck her ear like a fist. That tiny, horrified voice in her mind grew louder. "Lucy Snow," it screamed, "what *have* you done?"

When they reached the edge of the crowd, the policemen slowed down. They walked over to the black van that waited across the street behind its two patient horses. One of the officers opened the rear door.

Lucy spoke her first words since the police had reached her. She swallowed hard and said, in hushed tones, "You're not going to put me in there, are you?"

"It's the usual way we transport prisoners to jail, Miss," said one policeman. His voice was gentle, but the words were a knife that cut deep.

She had been arrested like a common criminal.

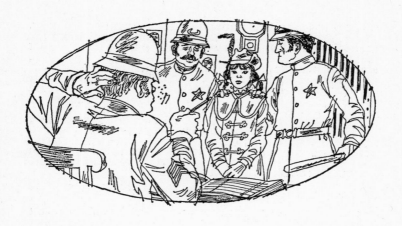

XXVI

THE INSIDE of the van was dark. The only light came through the small, barred opening at one end, and all Lucy could see was the back of the driver's neck. The bench that ran along the side was hard and splintery. Slivers stuck her fingers. A stale odor stung her nose.

She braced herself as the van swayed around the corner, but the gesture was automatic. This was not Lucy Snow riding off to jail; it must be some poor creature who lived down near Smith's Hollow, a fallen girl from one of those families that the church was always having to feed and clothe. Such things just didn't happen to the Snows.

Gradually her eyes adjusted to the dim light, and she

could see two forms slumped on the bench opposite her. One of them leaned forward and, with a breath that reeked of whiskey, said, "This your first offense, Lady?"

Lucy drew back from the fumes. "Yes," she said slowly. "What . . . what will they do to me?"

"Depends . . . depends on what you're charged with," said the man. The words were thick and each one was borne on a cloud of alcohol.

"I'm not sure. I climbed on the stage when Senator Throckmorton was speaking and told them what a liar he was."

"Ohhhhhh." The man put his finger to his lips. "That's very serious. Me and my friend here will go home in the morning, but you . . ." He scratched his head. "You won't get more than a month at hard labor."

A month at hard labor! She wondered what kind of hard labor women performed. They couldn't work on the road gang with picks and shovels. Perhaps they spent their time boiling laundry in some hot, steamy kitchen. That was the hardest work Mother had to do.

The driver reined in the horses and the motion stopped. There was a screech of metal as someone drew back the iron bolt. The door swung open and a voice called, "Come out, miss."

Lucy got to her feet and edged toward the opening. As she put her foot on the first step, a hand steadied her. She walked toward the police station between two officers, each with a firm grip on one of her arms. Their grasp was no tighter than Tom's had been, but their touch seemed cruel and harsh.

Behind her the two drunks stumbled along, kept on their feet by the prodding of nightsticks.

Lucy looked around the shabby station. Beside a desk stood a tarnished brass spittoon. Splotches of tobacco juice on the floor testified to the poor marksmanship of the police force.

An officer sat beside a glowing potbellied stove. His cap was tipped forward on his head and his hands were folded across his round belly. At the sound of their footsteps, he sat up and adjusted his uniform.

"Another load of drunks?" he asked sleepily. When he realized that Lucy was among the prisoners, his eyes widened. "What's the charge?"

"Creating a public disturbance," said one of the officers. The hard words seemed to slap against the wall.

To hear her defense of truth described in the cold language of the law sent a chill down Lucy's spine. When Bill Masters had ridden his horse through the town, firing a gun into the air as fast as he could put bullets in it, Father had called it a "public disturbance." It wasn't the same at all.

The policeman sighed and walked over to the desk. He drew a large book to him and dipped a pen in the inkwell.

"Name?" he asked.

"Lucy . . . Lucy Snow, sir," she said, her voice quavering.

"Where do you live?"

"236 Elm Street."

"Oh, you're Will Snow's daughter." The pen scratched busily. "Never expected to see you in here, young lady."

As he wrote down the details of her crime, she wondered when they would thrust her into a cold, bare cell, when the judge would rap his gavel and sentence her to prison. A month at hard labor!

The policeman scratched his head and frowned. "I don't know what I'm going to do with you," he said.

He glanced at the officers who stood on either side of Lucy. "The cells are full of drunks," he said, "there's no place to put her." He shook his head. "You know what it's been like today. There's been a quart of whiskey guzzled for every skyrocket fired."

There was a long silence, broken only by the sound of her racing heart. Then one of the officers leaned over and whispered in the ear of the man behind the desk. They talked together quietly and Lucy could not catch their words. She wondered what they were plotting. Would they send her directly to prison because the jail was full?

"Just sit there by the stove, Miss," the policeman said

at last. "We'll figure out something when the chief comes back." He waved toward the back door and spoke to the officers. "Put those drunks in the tank to sleep it off. There must be some room left on the floor."

On legs that trembled Lucy walked over to the chair and sat stiffly on the edge of the seat. The officers took the befuddled prisoners out of the room. After the door shut behind them, Lucy remained rigid, hardly daring to breathe. Perhaps if she made no noise, the policeman would forget that she was there.

She looked straight ahead, at a board covered with "wanted" posters. The hard eyes that stared back at her no longer belonged to creatures who lived in a distant world. Lucy Snow was now one of them.

What would happen when she finally got out of jail — a convicted criminal? She saw herself disowned by her family and friends. She wondered if Tom would ever speak to her again. Perhaps he would cross to the other side of the street as she passed. She would hear Father say, "I had a daughter once, but we don't speak of her anymore." Perhaps, like Aunt Letitia, she would have to leave town. She could see herself slinking through the dirty streets of a city slum, a bag of stolen silver on her back. It was clear that a life of crime awaited her — and all because she dared to challenge the slave masters of society. The thought of her unjust treatment gave her some kind of painful pleasure.

The slamming of a door pulled her back to the dingy room. Striding toward her was Aunt Letitia, a determined look on her face. Behind her was Jonathan Harrison. Without a word to the policeman, her aunt drew up a chair and sat beside her.

"Are you all right, Lucy?" she asked. "We saw them take you away and we got here as fast as we could. Your father is coming along. There was such a crowd around the dray that he couldn't get the horses moving."

At her aunt's concern the painful joys of martyrdom fled. Lucy was once more a frightened girl. "I . . . I suppose they're going to send me to jail," she said. With her knuckle she dashed a tear from the corner of her eye. "I'm charged with creating a public disturbance."

"I don't think you have to worry about jail," said Aunt Letitia. She patted her hand. "Not during an election campaign." She smiled. "They're always afraid of bad publicity just before the vote is taken."

"Keep your chin up," said Mr. Harrison. A warm smile creased his face. "You mustn't lose heart. Letitia is counting on you to help organize the women of New York. We're going to open a special office for woman suffrage down at the store."

Before Lucy could answer the station door burst open and Father rushed in. He almost ran to the desk and demanded to see the police chief.

"Sorry, Will," said the officer, "he's down at the park."

"You are detaining my daughter," said Father, out of breath, "and I demand her release."

"She's right over there," said the officer. He pointed at Lucy. "But I can't release her yet. She's charged with creating a public disturbance."

For the first time Father realized that Lucy was in the room. He took one step toward her, then — as his glance fell upon Aunt Letitia — he stopped. He stared at her. Then, with a curt "I suppose you put her up to this," he turned his back on his sister and put his hand on Lucy's shoulder.

"Are you all right?" he stammered. "Have they harmed you in any way?"

"No one hurt me, Father," she said. "But I'm so glad to see you."

"We'll have you out of here in no time," he said. He looked down at her and his face became stern. "What a fool thing to do," he said. "I thought my daughter had a little horse sense."

Before she could reply, the door burst open and Senator Throckmorton hurried into the room. He waddled to the desk, followed by Judge Clark and Mr. Bryan and three men from the train.

"I understand you're holding that girl who jumped up on the stage," said the Senator. His voice had lost the mellowness that mesmerized crowds; it was harsh and edgy.

Lucy shrank back in her chair. He might ask them

to keep her in jail until after the election next month. She was sure that the police would do whatever the distinguished visitor asked.

Like the dawning of the sun, a smile broke across Father's face and he stepped toward the desk. Just like a man, thought Lucy. His only daughter at the prison gates and he fawns over a walrus from Washington.

"Thank God you've come, Senator," he said.

The Senator brushed aside his greeting and pounded on the desk. "I want that girl released immediately," he shouted. "I refuse to prefer any charges."

"Yes, sir," said the policeman, now alert. He picked up the pen and began to write. "If you refuse to press charges," he said, "we can't hold her any longer." He looked at Father and Lucy. "Guess you can take her home, Will," he said. "Just keep her off public platforms."

The Senator shook Father's hand. "Mr. Snow," he said, the sharp edge gone from his voice, "you certainly are raising a flock of politicians." He smiled at Lucy. "But this young suffragist is a little embarrassing."

"We're going to have a talk when we get home," said Father.

"Next time you give a speech, young lady," said the Senator, "be sure you've been invited." He bowed over Lucy's hand. "It's the best way to stay out of jail."

Lucy gave a tiny, stiff smile, but said nothing. She was sorry she had been arrested, but she doubted that suffragists would ever be invited to speak in Smithville.

While the Senator talked to Lucy, Aunt Letitia kept her eyes on Judge Clark. She put her hand on his sleeve. "You might at least say hello, Henry," she said.

"How do you do, Letitia," he said. The frown lines between his eyes deepened. "It has been years since we met."

"More than twenty-five since we went for a ride in your buggy," said Aunt Letitia. She looked as if she were enjoying the Judge's discomfort. "I thought we might meet before this."

"I had heard you were visiting your brother," he said stiffly.

"I've been visiting for nearly two weeks," said Aunt Letitia.

"I'm a busy man." The Judge looked from side to side begging to be rescued. "I hope your stay has been pleasant. A suffragette faces a cold welcome in this town." He brushed past her.

"Perhaps. But Jonathan Harrison tells me that after we're married people might change their minds."

The Judge stopped and slowly turned around. "After you're married? To Jonathan Harrison?" His expression changed as if an electric switch had been thrown. "Jonathan Harrison's wife is always welcome."

"It's good of you to say that, Henry," said Mr. Harrison, "but there was never any thought that she would not be welcome."

Now Judge Clark saw the department store owner standing behind Aunt Letitia. "Well . . . but . . . I mean . . ." He groped for words.

Aunt Letitia broke in. "Still judging by the surface, Henry? Is it all right to be a suffragette and a scarlet woman if you're married to the biggest merchant in town?"

"I don't know what you're talking about," said the Judge frostily.

Before he could utter another word, the Senator tugged at his sleeve. "We're late for the meeting," he said.

As they walked away, Aunt Letitia grinned. "I intend to embarrass that pompous jackass at every opportunity," she said. "And before I'm through with him, he'll be after the Senator to sponsor woman suffrage." She looked at Father. "There's nothing more I can do here."

Father stared at her.

"Goodbye, Aunt Letitia," said Lucy. "Thank you for helping to rescue me. And goodbye . . . Uncle Jonathan." The word came with only slight hesitation. "Thank you for helping."

Senator Throckmorton and his committee followed Aunt Letitia and Uncle Jonathan out the door. As he left, the Senator glanced back over his shoulder.

"Why didn't one of you tell me this town was a nest of suffragettes?" he asked Judge Clark. The edge was back in his voice. "I'd never have given that fool speech."

The banging of the door cut off the Judge's reply.

XXVII

The ride home from the police station was quiet. Only the clop-clop of the horses' hoofs broke the stillness of the night. The streets were deserted and between the glow of the gas lamps, darkness swallowed the dray and its silent passengers.

Both Father and Lucy kept their eyes on the road, as if some awful hazard might appear. From time to time Father stole glances at his daughter, each time shaking his head in disbelief.

The silence grew until it seemed there was a high brick wall between them, but Lucy could not say the word that would break it down. Only a few weeks ago, Father would have joked and teased. The sounds of laughter would have followed the dray all the way home. Tonight, two strangers rode side by side on the cold and narrow seat.

The moment the horses pulled into the yard, Lucy slid down and ran into the house. She hoped to slip up the stairs and into her room without meeting anyone, but as she hurried Mother came out of the parlor.

"Lucy!" she said and held out her arms.

Safe inside Mother's warm embrace, Lucy felt the tears gather. In another second she would be sobbing aloud.

The slamming of the kitchen door twisted in her stomach. The tears froze and dry-eyed, she turned to face Father.

"I think we'd better have a talk," he said. There was no warmth in his voice.

Lucy and Mother followed him into the parlor. No fire had burned that day and the room was cold. But the shiver that came over Lucy had nothing to do with the temperature.

Father stood in the center of the flowered carpet, his feet planted wide apart, his hands clasped behind his back. "My father would have given me a good hiding for what you did tonight," he said.

Lucy's glance darted about the room. She forced herself to look squarely at Father. Inside she was trembling and it took all her strength to keep from dropping her eyes to the floor.

He sighed. "I suppose you're too big to be whipped,"

he said. "But you've disgraced the Snow name."

"I'm sorry, Father," said Lucy. "I didn't intend to." Her voice was so faint that he had to lean forward to catch her words.

"Didn't intend," said Father. "That's the whole trouble, you never intend. You act without thinking of the consequences." He warmed to his lecture. "You made a public spectacle of yourself and shamed your mother and me."

"The charges were dropped," she whispered.

"So they were." He twisted his mustache. "But the Senator could have preferred charges," he said, "and then where would you be? Behind bars, I'll be bound."

"He said things that weren't true," she said. Her voice grew stronger. "He lied."

"And that gave you the right to act like a crazy woman?" asked Father. "That was his rally. The Republican Party paid for the lights and the fireworks and the barbecue and the parade. You had no business on that stage."

Lucy sorted desperately through her mind for something that would excuse her. A fragment from a civics lesson turned up and she grasped it. "I was exercising my freedom of speech," she said.

"By denying the Senator his freedom?" said Father. "By insulting a United States Senator? That doesn't make good sense."

He paced back and forth in the narrow space between the sofa and the big chair. Lucy waited for his next words. She feared the worst was yet to come. Father had not yet decided what to do with her.

Suddenly he whirled on her and his voice was crosser than before. "It was bad enough when you passed out leaflets," he shouted. "That at least was orderly. But I will not stand for this kind of — of — of violent disruption." He shook his finger in her face. "As long as you're under my roof . . ."

During the argument Mother had stepped to his side. She laid her hand on his arm and he stopped in midsentence. He dropped his finger and began again, this time in a softer voice.

"I want you to promise me," he said, "that you will keep all your activities within the bounds of the law." Again he chewed on his mustache.

Lucy relaxed. This would be easier than she expected. "I promise," she said. "I didn't mean to break the law tonight, Father. I was on that stage before I knew what I was doing."

Father raised an eyebrow. "Perhaps," he said. "But just to make sure that you're not carried away again, I want you to come straight home after school for the next three weeks. By that time the election will be over."

Her shoulders slumped. "Yes, Father," she said in a tiny voice.

She turned and walked slowly out of the parlor and up the stairs. Sam's door opened and he tiptoed out on his bare feet, his nightshirt flapping around his legs.

"Did they put you behind bars?" he asked. "Did they take your fingerprints?"

"No," said Lucy. "Your friend the Senator made them let me go." She tried to push past Sam but he followed her.

"I never saw Father so mad," he said. "I hope he never gets that mad at me."

She paused, her hand on the doorknob. "I have to come straight home after school and stay in the house for the next three weeks," she said. "That's what you wanted to find out, isn't it?"

Sam whistled. "Three weeks!" he said. "That's past Halloween. I'd rather have a licking any day than miss Halloween."

"Halloween is for children," said Lucy in her haughtiest voice.

Sam trudged back to his room and slammed the door. Before Lucy could go inside, there was a loud knocking downstairs. She waited in the hall, listening as Father went to answer it.

There stood Tom's father and before he could step over the threshold, he asked about Lucy.

"She's home and she's safe," said Father. "Thank you for getting the Senator down to the station so fast."

"It must have been a terrible experience for her," said Mr. Bryan. "Maybe it cured her of politics."

"Not my daughter," said Father. He chuckled.

"That girl has spunk. If women ever do get the vote, she'll be the Governor of New York."

Lucy went into her room in a daze. The pride in Father's voice could not be hidden. Suddenly the gulf between them seemed only half as wide.

XXVIII

Lucy had scarcely settled herself behind her desk when Miss Austen told her to report to the principal's office. She could not imagine why Mr. Amberson wanted to see her, and the small knot in her stomach grew larger with each step she took down the corridor.

She reached the end of the hall and studied the brass plate on the door. For the fifth time she read the words, LLEWELLYN P. AMBERSON, PRINCIPAL, now as deeply engraved in her mind as they were on the polished metal. She drew a last, large breath, opened the door and walked in.

The principal sat behind his desk, his head bent over a stack of papers, his bald pate shining in the sunlight that streamed through the window. Lucy waited, telling herself there was nothing to fear, and at last he looked up from beneath his shaggy eyebrows.

The knot suddenly felt like a cannonball. Mr. Amberson's eyes were not sparkling with kindness this morning; they seemed to glitter with all the fervor of Long John Silver just before he ordered a victim to walk the plank.

"Good morning, Miss Snow," he said in a polite but forbidding voice. "Please sit down." He waved at a hard, straight chair that stood beside the desk.

"Good morning," said Lucy. She sat down gingerly and remembered to place her feet together as Mother always reminded her to do. She smoothed her skirt nervously as she waited for the principal to speak.

He twisted the bushy hairs of his eyebrow, just as Father sometimes twisted his mustache. After a moment he said, "That was a bad business Saturday night, a bad business."

She was determined not to help. "Sir?" she said.

"Why," he said, "starting a ruckus in the park and being carried off to jail like a common thief. It could hardly be called a good business." He tugged at his eyebrow.

"No, sir," said Lucy. She stared at his busy fingers, caught as always by the magnitude of his bristling brows. She was sure that if she laid a pencil across that hairy shelf, it would rest as securely as on a table.

"Two members of the school board paid me a call this

morning before breakfast," he said. "They were deeply disturbed that an officer of Smithville High School had been arrested."

He clamped his lips together. If he could only see inside, he would find a mass of quivering jelly, but she hid her fear behind a steady gaze.

After a moment he cleared his throat. At the rumbling sound, Lucy stiffened. Father always cleared his throat noisily when he had anything unpleasant to say. She clasped her hands tightly together but said nothing.

"I must remove you from the office of ninth grade secretary," he said, biting off each word. "We cannot have a law breaker leading our students."

Father's punishment was nothing beside this. It wasn't fair! She had climbed upon that stage for only a minute. And he was going to take away a whole year's excitement and honor in return.

"You . . ." The sound in her throat was only a croak. She swallowed and began again. "You can't do that."

"Indeed I can," said Mr. Amberson, "and I have." His eyes softened. "I'm truly sorry, Lucy, but I have no choice."

"But why?" she asked. "I didn't hurt anyone. I objected only when the Senator said things that weren't true. And the charges were dismissed. I wasn't convicted or put in jail." Her cheeks grew very pink. "You're only doing this because you don't want women

184

to have the vote." Her voice grew shrill. "You're just like all men."

The principal pulled at his eyebrow again and sighed. "You forget," he said, "that class officers must set an example for the rest of the students. That's why we require them to have good grades. And," he continued, "that's why we cannot have an officer who has been arrested. The students will think that if you don't have to obey the laws, neither do they."

The chair legs screeched on the polished floor as Lucy suddenly stood up. "May I go?" she asked.

Mr. Amberson slowly nodded. "Yes," he said, "but I wish you'd try to understand. It really has nothing to do with the way I feel about woman suffrage."

She turned and walked quickly out of the office, slamming the door behind her. She was determined not to cry in front of the principal. All the way back to the classroom, she dragged her feet. Inside the students were conjugating a Latin verb aloud; she could hear them chanting the past tense.

She couldn't open the door and go in. Tears were still close to the surface. Everyone could tell by looking at her that something dreadful had happened. She waited in the corridor until the bell rang for recess.

Tom was one of the first to leave the room. He hurried over to Lucy and they walked down the hall together.

"What did Mr. Amberson want?" he asked.

"Nothing much," said Lucy. She took a deep breath. "It seems they don't want criminals as class officers."

"What criminal is Mr. Amberson after?" he asked.

"Me," she said. "I'm the dangerous convict of Smithville High. And I've just been stripped of my office. You see, I might corrupt the students." She kept up a brave smile, but the corners of her mouth trembled.

Tom scowled. "That's terrible," he said. "Let's go someplace where we can talk."

They walked down the steps and over to the great elm that shaded a corner of the school yard. With his handkerchief Tom brushed off the bench that stood beneath it.

"Now," he said when they were seated, "tell me what happened — and don't leave out anything."

Lucy repeated her entire conversation with Mr. Amberson. Then she leaned back and waited for Tom to speak.

He studied his shoe for a long time before he said a word. Then he looked up and said, "It's a dirty shame, but there's nothing you can do about it."

"Only an awful man would act like that," said Lucy.

One at a time, slowly, the words came out. "He didn't have any choice," Tom said.

Lucy jumped to her feet. She couldn't even depend upon Tom. "Just like a man," she said. "You're all alike. The minute a woman stands up for her rights, you band together and drag her down."

Tom grabbed her hands and pulled her back to the bench. "Lucy Snow," he said, "your temper matches your hair. And that's a good part of your trouble. Now you listen to me for a minute."

He kept both her hands trapped in his so that she couldn't move. She turned her head to show that she wanted no part of this conversation.

"Look at me," he said.

Slowly, ever so slowly, she pulled back her gaze until their eyes met.

"That's better," said Tom. "It seems to me that you were fighting mad over those men who interrupted your aunt a couple of weeks ago. If it was wrong for them to stop her, why is it right for you to stop the Senator?"

"But . . ." said Lucy, "but he was telling lies. And I didn't throw any eggs." She had never thought of her own escapade as anything like that other terrible night.

"So you didn't throw any eggs," he said. "Good for you. But the result was the same. They stopped Aunt Letitia and you stopped the Senator. Neither one of them had a fair chance. And I'll bet those egg throwers thought Aunt Letitia was telling lies."

Lucy shifted uneasily on the bench. "Maybe it was wrong to interrupt him," she said faintly. Back to her mind rushed the memory of that tiny voice screaming silent warnings as she charged the stage. "But who listens to a woman in this town? It was the only way I could tell them."

"Maybe it was," said Tom. "In that case, how deeply do you believe in women's rights? Are they really important to you?"

Hadn't he paid any attention at all to what she had done? Didn't he realize the trouble she'd had at home because it was so important to her? She tossed her head. "Of course I believe in women's rights," she said.

"Then take your medicine like a man," he said. Suddenly he grinned. "No offense intended. Lots of suffragists have gone to jail for the cause. And they took their punishment without complaint."

No one had ever talked like this to her before. And she had never stopped to think; as fast as thoughts came into her mind, she acted. "I guess," she said slowly, "that unless a cause is worth a sacrifice, it's not very important."

Tom kept silent. His grip relaxed until his clasp was gentle. He waited. His eyes were on her face.

"Oh, Tom," she said, "I'm going to miss being a class officer with you this year."

He squeezed her hand. "We'll be so busy working for votes for women," he said, "that you'll never miss it."

The clanging of the school bell called an end to recess. Arm in arm they walked slowly across the yard.

"I've been thinking," said Tom. "It just might be fun to be the husband of the Governor of New York."

Together they climbed the steps, and together they entered the big front door.